Midnight In Footscray

Frank T Bird

For the Lamas, who go around pretending not to enjoy everything.

No One Gives A Fuck Anymore

I woke up on this shitty bench.

I must have passed out in this damn heat.

If I was Forrest Gump, this is where I'd start ranting about how I became a billionaire selling shrimp and investing in apples, but it's not like that.

Twenty-four hours ago, I was in a Parisian night suit with a rip in the anus, getting reamed by a furry hippo in lipstick called Arsehole Taylor, using Black and Gold polyunsaturated margarine as lube. And yeah, it *is* better for the cholesterol. Thanks for asking.

The blokes called him Arsehole Taylor because he liked arse-holes, and he *was* one. That's what I'll tell people when they ask about my time in the gaff. It's romantic. I've been working on it for a while.

You're the first I've told about this. I'm *Meth Gump*. Do you see that off-white feather that just landed on my boot? It's the same colour as the Sydney Opera House.

And yeah, I fucked up a waiter because he gave me a butter knife to cut sourdough. What a prick, right? Him, I mean, not me. Everyone knows a butter knife is too blunt to cut sourdough. You need something meaner, sharper, more serrated. This prick wants me to fling my toast at some fat-lipped professor because I can't control my knife. Would you ask Zorro to go into battle with a — I don't know — a blunt sword?

So now you think I'm some fucking psycho, but it's not like that either. I was just in a bad place. Anyone could have gotten what the waiter got. It wasn't personal. That's what I told him as he bled out on the floor.

And now I've got an irrational fear of bread. I mean, it's only mild. It's not like I run out of the room when there's bread. It's more of a reminder of what has been. My preferred carb is rice. *Fuck* bread.

I'm not just changing the subject here, either. The connection is that I beat the shit out of him. It's why I'm on this hot bench —my first day out in six months.

It's what they call *justice*.

It's twenty-past-five, and my ride isn't here yet. When I say my ride, I mean the bus. There's no actual ride to speak of. You don't get rides after six months. Rides are for hardheads doing life for robbing Las Vegas casinos.

I wish I had a hat. My head is cooking like a bald soufflé, and I'm sweating like a Black Iberian on performance-enhancing drugs.

The bus has arrived, and it stinks. Now I have to jog up the stairs like I ride buses all the time, and I still have a zest for life.

There's whispering — especially two women in the back seat. They know this bus stop. It's where all the hardheads, just released, get the bus. They're probably wondering what I did. They're probably wondering if I shot my uncle or —

"Come on, Mate, move it." It's Anaemic Shrek, the driver.

I hand him the chalky ticket, and he rips it in half. When I turn back to the crowd, no one gives a fuck anymore. They've all gone back to staring out the window, dreaming of their next shot of GBH or the correct number of onions in a traditional mince and potato flange. Fuck knows what a flange is. I just made it up.

I hate buses. Trains I can handle — and trams — but there's something depressing about buses. Happy people are rare on buses because it's the lowest of the low. If you're riding a bus, someone shat in your potatoes, Mate. You're right down there.

Not one smile. Not one look to say,

I'm a human. You're a human. Let's breathe the same rancid air for forty-four minutes.

No one gives a fuck anymore.

The air on this bus is warm and musky, like having your head buried deep in a pussy. The deranged weatherman: Today will be humid, with a thirty-two per cent chance of crabs.

On the subject of love, it's twelve complete moon cycles since my wife's head came apart like an organic nashi pear under the rear left wheel of an ultramarine Ford Maverick. And don't freak out, alright? I know I just sprung that on you, but it was bound to come out eventually.

I'm not even sure why I told you. I suppose it's so you don't think I'm the kind of person that randomly attacks waiters.

I suppose I must *care* what you think about me.

Fuck it.

I once watched a YouTube video where this ex-convict called Ted told people that dropping the soap in prison was a myth. Ted was wrong, that prick. It's *not* a myth. Bars of soap get dropped every day, and you can't do anything about it because you're too afraid to die bleeding out in a prison hospital. It's just *easier* to die from too much criminal spunk up the potty.

The hum of this bus is sickening. It's like someone has eaten a power tool, and it's going off inside their stomach — low, muffled vibration like a deranged chi machine. *Fuck buses.*

We're still in the country — all green fields and animals. There's a sheep with a bird on its back. Is that a sign? Maybe. Or maybe it's just a bird on a sheep's back.

There was this inmate called Mike Jagger. He hated it when people called him Mick. And he was no Rolling Stone — whatever the fuck that means.

People think you've got to be physically big to win a fight, but that's not true. You've got to be big in the mind. The most important question is, *who is willing to go further?* You can have a stinging right hook, but if you aren't ready to kill your opponent, you're weak.

Mike Jagger was willing to do anything — rip your nutsack off — jam his thumbs in your eyes — bite you all over, crunching his teeth through your fingers like a bloody Twix without hesitation. He's small, but no one touches Mike. Because, if you're fighting Mike, you'll have to kill the fucker. And most prisoners don't want to kill. They want to go home and smoke weed on their couch. Life just rear-ended them on the wrong day, and they reacted. Now they find themselves surrounded by violent criminals in cramped conditions.

It's a *thinking man's* rehabilitation.

It worked for me. I'll do just about anything not to go back there. I'd be Harrison Ford getting pursued by that Tommy Lee from Motley Crue across the crocodile plains. I'd throw myself off a building before I let them take me back.

I'm not even joking.

The fucking hum is still going. Fucking power tool. Just digest it already. I'd get out and walk, but I'm only eighteen minutes in — twenty-sixish to go.

The girl across from me is too cute to be on this bus. I point to the graffiti above her head that says *fat cunts*. And I say something like,

"Pretty rude, eh?"

She ignores me.

At the same time, I notice I'm sitting on a brown stain, only it's dry and flakey, and all you can do is hope it's Coke, not Kak, as in *Kaka Kola*.

I want to tell her this, but I can't figure out the words, so I ask her what she's reading instead, but I say it as quiet as a mouse in a library, and there's no way she can hear me. She's not fucking Spiderman or whatever.

I don't really want a conversation anyway. I just want her to acknowledge my presence and say,

I'm a human. You're a human. Let's breathe the same pungent air for another twenty-four and a half minutes.

No one gives a fuck anymore.

There's a woman four seats up with a dog that looks like a pit bull, so I go over and ask if I can pat the dog. She tells me his name is Charlie and that he loves pats. I tickle Charlie's face, and he licks mine. I get a damn lump in my throat, and tears come. I didn't want this grief. I just wanted to pat a dog.

We *had* a dog. But none of us was available anymore — my wife being dead and me being an inmate — so he got sent to a pound, where they stuck a needle of green shit in him. No one would have taken him because he was too old. I let him down, and that feels like a ball of molten metal in the middle of my chest.

Charlie's owner asks if I'm alright. She's got a deranged ginger perm and a purple shell suit. Her lipstick is really fucking red like she's been sucking off Elmo.

"I'm fine. I just had a dog like yours once," I tell her.

Damn it, Charlie. I was doing just fine till you came along.

I return to my seat, and things are getting semi-industrial. We're in the Western suburbs now, and there's a much denser population of poor people than in the imperialist East where I used to live. I was trained in the ways of the imperialists from a young age — *private all-boys*. After that, I was all CK suits, scotch and money — until the shit show.

The point is, I'm a fucking prawn out of water on this side of town. Where are the stinking middle class dipping their genitals in the avocado puree with lobster butter or whatever? It's not that I miss them or anything. I just feel a little out of place.

"Mini Orsis," says this weird guy sitting at the back. He looks like Rick Stein without teeth. He nods his head out of the window and looks back at me.

"Mini Orsis," he says again, pointing out the window.

I spot the miniature horses. At first, they're real cute, with their fluffy heads and tiny legs. Then I notice their dicks are a foot of rope, and that's not even stiff — not even a bit stiff.

Charlie's owner has a good look. She seems like the type that might fuck a miniature horse. I don't mean that to be derogatory. We're all just one car crash away from fucking a miniature horse.

I reckon I could convince myself to fuck a miniature horse or at least let them fuck me while Charlie's owner watched. Not Charlie, though. I can't stand it when dogs watch you fuck. They just look like they are enjoying it too much.

❖

I give Charlie one last pat on the way off the gastrointestinal power tool and step down into the lower intestine of society.

Footscray station is a stinking arsehole of a place, and I'm shitting a brick. I'm starting again fresh. I'm like a newborn baby in this world — innocent, pink, sensitive skin — ready to cry at anything.

There's a shitty phone box covered in graffiti and a dried substance that could easily be *Kaka Kola*. I negotiate the brown crustacean and take a moment to bypass the temptation to follow the order on the phone box wall, which says, *for a good fuck, call Samir.*

I call the number on my discharge summary instead, and this social worker called Keith says he can come to pick me up. I tell him I'd rather walk, but he insists, so I tell him I'm at Footscray station, and he starts going on about some noodle place opposite. I want to tell him I just got out of the gaff, and noodles are the last thing on my mind, but I don't since the guy is putting me up. Still, he keeps talking. Is this prick on speed?

Footscray seems alright, I suppose. There are *a lot* of Muslims, though. I think that's alright. I'm fairly sure our enemies are Russia and China these days. Or, at least, they were six months ago. I'll have to check the newspapers.

And no, I'm not some bright young skinhead like Russell Crowe in Romper Stomper, if that's what you're thinking. Sure, the illegal spunk of racism *is* well-established in my rectum. I was *information-ally raped* from an early age, but I'm working on it, alright?

I shuffle past all the dirty taxis to the noodle shop this Keith fucker told me about. The shop stinks like a homeless guy's underpants. It should be called *Rectums and Coriander*. Is that racist? I don't think so. If anything, it's herbism. Thankfully, the stench is from a grid outside the shop. It's not the smell of noodles.

Some Greek-looking man is smoking, and I want to ask him for a cigarette, but I'm terrified. I'm still in the East in my office, ignoring my wife, making sweet love to an Excel spreadsheet and drinking scotch mixed with Gaviscon — too good to ask for help and too rich to ask for a cigarette. I have seven dollars and fifty-five cents, and it's not 1981.

Some fucker is tapping my shoulder. I spin around to see a sick-looking bastard with brown teeth and spew coating his Marilyn Manson t-shirt and a hole where his nose used to be. He asks me for change, and I tell him to fuck off, primarily out of fear.

I back into this old lady, causing her to drop her purse and coins all over the ground. So, now I'm apologising like Hugh Grant and picking these filthy coins up off the wretched pavement. But why? How did this happen? Who uses coins these days anyway?

I give her the coins back, expecting thanks, but she mutters something and fucks off. I'm glad. I caused her the shit in the first place. Why would she say thanks? It's *justice*.

The noseless man has fucked off, too. He is over by the Greek bloke who also tells him to fuck off, only louder and more aggressively, and without taking out a pensioner. I should be taking notes.

I'm feeling anxious as fuck as I head past the motorised Joni Mitchell Big Bird taxis to a caravan at the bottom of the station steps. They sell chips, burgers, hot dogs — that kind of crap. I ask the guy for water, and he gives me a look like I asked to finger his daughter. Then he hands me a bottle, and I give him three dollars of my seven odd. It's fucking expensive for a bit of water. Sixty per cent of my body is made from this shit. *Why don't I just drink myself?*

I take a couple of deep breaths. There's a lot of plastic wrapped around this tiny bit of water. I don't want to think about these things, but the thoughts keep coming. I can't stop the thoughts. They'll *never* stop. I can't control them. Some fucker is pouring hot and cold water over me simultaneously, and here comes the panic, like the school bully coming across the field. *Fuck.*

There's a lame toot, and I swing around. Some greasy fucker is waving at me from a shit-cream Ford Falcon. Or maybe he's waving at someone else. Maybe that's the guy — Keith.

I drink more water, but it's too cold and feels like a metal pipe in my throat. I'm sweating like a bastard, and he's getting out of the car.

Fuck.

Now, I'm running in the other direction.

This is the bit where Meth Gump can't handle what is happening, so he runs around the country.

I don't know why. I just felt like running.

Run Meth, RUN.

At some stage, I realise I have to go back so I don't get lost and have to sleep on these greasy streets. I feel a bit better, anyway. Running always helps.

I *think* I'm okay until I pass an aquarium and stop to tap on the window at the poor fuckers trapped in their tanks. Things can always be worse. Aren't we just like fish? Aren't we this drop of consciousness trapped in the body?

The claustrophobia is kicking in like a lousy pill now, and I want to escape my body. The hot and cold water is rushing again, and I shake my head, running across the road and away from the station *again*.

This is fucking ridiculous. I *have* to go back.

Keith, the social worker, is leaning against the shit-cream Falcon, flicking his greasy black-grey hair and smiling like a sex offender. He's wearing a faded Hawaii Five-O shirt with one of those spiked belts, and his arse is way too small. You can't trust a man with a tiny arse. Still, it matches the rest of his body which looks like he hasn't eaten in a year or two.

I don't care about any of it. I'm too busy staring at the cigarette in his hand.

◆

This prick needs to clean up his car. I'm sitting among McDonald's bags and shit. Then again, at least I can breathe into them in the event of another flip-out. The smell of genetically modified canola oil always calms me down.

The inside of this car smells like cheese, and not the good type either. It's not aged cheddar or Red Leicester or King Island double cream brie.

It's the type of cheese that collects in places — the thirty-day-old pot of yoghurt — *human cheese, thrush. Dick cheese.*

Whatever you want to call it, it's sour and unpleasant.

The cigarette smoke makes it mildly better. I'd call it a carcinogenic air freshener, but all air fresheners are carcinogenic, including cheese-flavoured Christmas trees.

Humans are fucking hogs. We evolved to use toiletries to disguise it, but if hogs and dogs used deodorant, we might think they were civilised animals too. Truth is, none of us are. We are as horrific as any other creature. We just have Speedstick.

"How you doin, Pal?" Keith asks. He sounds like Ray Winstone on helium, and it's the kind of question asked in the kind of tone you don't need following a panic attack.

"Fine," I tell him, staring out of the window. I've got nothing else. I suck down on the cheap cigarette he gave me. It's called a *Longbeach*.

Surely there's something else to say. I'm not Julian Assange. I'm a damn free citizen.

Say something, for fuck's sake.

"How much is a packet of ciggies these days?" I ask like I'm Ariana Huffington at some social event. It's just something to say, damn it. We need to connect. I'm starting again fresh, like a newborn baby — innocent, pink and all that crap.

"Depends on the brand," he tells me. "I smoke these — Longbeach. Forty for sixty bucks, they are. Yer quality shit though, like yer Marlboros — talking twenty-five for fifty bucks."

I'm trying to think of something to say next to keep this shit going so I don't have to listen to these damn thoughts, but I don't know what the fuck he is talking about because I only started smoking in the last six months.

"Fifty bucks, eh?" I say, and there's an uncomfortable pause.

"I smoked chop-chop in the gaff," I tell him. He nods and flicks his ciggy end out of the window. Then he starts going on about the time he tried to grow chop-chop and got chased by a police helicopter. Fuck knows if he is lying.

Chop-chop is homegrown tobacco, in case you're wondering. It's more illegal than cocaine in Australia. You get life for growing enough of it. Fuck knows why. It's horrible. Smoking chop-chop is like sucking off a wasp. This cheap Longbeach is like Panama Gold in comparison — whatever that means.

There's No Place Called Home

The shit-cream Falcon pulls up on a tiny street outside this old red brick house. It's a no-frills kind of place. There are plenty of these on this side of town — faded lace blinds made with recycled old woman lingerie — manicured, brown grass and an unnecessary bush of psychotic thorns half blocking the path to the front door.

"Oh, watch the bush, Pal," Keith says as I puncture my thumb and scream like a little girl. I examine the bleeding hole while Keith rummages in his bag with a Longbeach hanging from his mouth like a skinny ape looking for fleas. He is ranting on *still* — something about figs or fags or —

"This month, it's you and this girl Astrid Pal. Couple of others," he says, changing the subject randomly, dropping his cigarette and still rummaging. I'm assuming he's talking about the other people who live here.

"You'll meet 'em all soon enough," he says. "The girl is the only one you need to bother about."

"Oh yeah, why's that then?" I ask.

After a lot of pissing around, Keith pulls out the key. He is hunched over like Ebenezer Scrooge, jangling his keys to unlock his front door and eat pea soup by the fire until Jacob Marley arrives, chained and filled with regret and —

"Rehab," he says. "She just got out of rehab, Pal."

Now he's got his hand on my chest.

"Look, Nick. She's a druggy, Pal. She doesn't need anything but ciggies — not even booze. You should also know she's a *nympho*." He glares into my eyes, waiting for some kind of response.

I shrug, wondering why he is telling me this and simultaneously wondering why this fucker doesn't keep his house key on his car key ring.

"She's brought back at least two guys this week," he says, glaring some more, and I shrug again.

I don't know what the fuck he expects me to say.

"It's against the rules, Pal. That's all I'm saying," he says.

He finally unlocks the damn door, and I follow him in, sucking on my bleeding thumb. I hope this bastard isn't gonna be counting the sex I'm gonna have — all *none* of it.

I ask *why he allows it*, and I'm being sarcastic, but he doesn't get it.

"Look, I'm not Adolf Hitler," he says.

He fucking looks a bit like him, though.

We walk up a brown-carpeted hallway, and there's this stench of incense like we've arrived in some fucking hippy commune. I like it. I honestly expected the smell of mince and potato flange.

The decor is *seventies whorehouse* — brown velvet curtains, cream wallpaper with faded orange cocks or birds or something like that. One door is thumping and chiming with drum and bass. That might be the resident nympho.

Keith shows me my room.

"Here it is," he says. "It's not much, but it's home."

He says it like he is Richard Landon in *Little House on the Prairie*, but if Landon was a skinny speed addict.

Little House on the Gear.

I don't mind his constant ampheta-dialogue because I don't feel like being alone with these damn thoughts. I want him to keep talking, and he obliges. It's perfect.

The room is a cliché — more cream walls, square, grey, reasonably comfortable carpet, old lady g-string blinds, double wooden built-in wardrobes with enough space to store a body on each shelf should I wish to do so.

"Yer got towels and stuff, I'm assuming?" Keith says.

I'm nodding, but I don't have towels and stuff. I can probably get some, though. I know a bloke on the inside who deals in towels and stuff.

Keith spends the next twenty-odd minutes giving the grand tour d'pimphole with many unnecessary details, such as how to set a timer on the washing machine, the best way to wash a juicer and how to start the mower just in case I fancied a mow — even though there is a paid gardener.

Keith reckons it's therapeutic — mowing, that is. I don't know if he's tricking me into doing it for free. I sort of get it.

He finishes by showing me his Thermomix, which he says cost eighteen hundred bucks but seems to be an expensive blender.

"Prize machine this is," he says, like some posh speedhead farmer showing off his best Berkshire pig.

Eventually, he leads me back to my cell, and I sit on the bed. When I say bed, I mean a mattress on the floor. Beds are for royalty and Hollywood actors.

"Happy Liberation Day," Keith says. He throws me a pack of forty Longbeach and a lighter, winks and leaves me alone with my damn thoughts.

He's alright, that skinny-arsed fucker. But now I'm sitting here, as numb as an Alaskan naturist and unsure how to proceed. I start by lighting up a Longbeach. Then, I consider my options.

I could have a wank, or I could have a drink. I'd like to run an algorithm to decide. There's probably an app for that kind of thing. There's an app for everything these days.

I log in to the imaginary app, and it says:

You've got no money to drink, so just have a wank instead.

Technology is amazing.

◈

Dinner was a real event when I was a kid. Dad was always like, *take yer elbows off the table, wash yer hands, don't talk to yer mother like that, finish yer potatoes.*

A shrink might say I overcompensated by eating in my room a lot later in life. I had my wife bring me food at my chafing station so I could keep courting meaningless Excel spreadsheets while mindlessly stuffing my ungrateful face with the steak and mash and gravy she'd spent hours making.

It didn't matter to me. I was the real fucking hero supporting the family. My one-word, mumbled thanks were the pinnacle of our contact after a while. Now I'd take an hour with Arsehole Taylor or a year with no legs or a life of no bollocks to see her come through that door and be able to say *thanks* like a dumb prick one more time.

The dinner bell rings.

Keith told me the dinner bell rings every evening at six thirty, and I thought he was joking. Now, I'm wondering if this is some kind of nunnery. Why the fuck is there a dinner bell? I don't like it. It's already too religious. Should I wear my habit for dinner, Sisters? I mean, I wouldn't want to get a curry stain on it, or God might smite me with his giant rainbow cock.

Keith had kindly explained that dinner was supplied each evening, but as it was buffet style, it was a choice. He didn't explain the dress code. Since there's a bell, I assume there is also a dress code.

Regardless, I like to wear a shirt when meeting new people. It's a hangover from my work days. I told Keith, and he dropped one in for me. Unfortunately, the shirt is deep purple, like the head of a fully erect cock, possibly inflated by a cock ring. I don't want to dress like a fully erect cock, but I've got nothing else, and I've had a shower — my first on the outside — so I'm feeling pure.

The drum and bass has stopped, and the drum and bass room door is open. I knock gently and peer into the room, but no one is home. The walls are covered in fractal posters and magic mushroom pictures. Down one end, there's some kind of shrine with a golden Buddha statue. It's the room of some mad fucking hippy.

"Can I help you?"

I almost leap out of my skin bag. I turn around, and I'm standing face to face with the mad hippy. She has purple hair that matches my cock-head shirt, and we both know it. Her skin is the pastiest white I've ever seen, and she is only wearing a black bra and tiny shorts. She definitely looks like a nympho, from what I've read. I mean, what is a nympho anyway? Two blokes a week — surely that's not —

My trance is broken by the palm of her right hand, which *smacks* me hard in the face. I'm shocked at how much it hurts, and tears come. Now, I look like a real fanny. I didn't expect this.

"I cut holes in the Swiss cheese once before a date to make it seem posher," I say. It's all that comes out, and I can't explain it.

She laughs like a nitrous whore. Then she stares at me, smiling.

I smile back through my tears.

She nods a few times like she is listening to an imaginary tune and spins around.

I follow her into the dining room, where everyone is eating what looks like testicle curry. There's some Christmas tablecloth, and it's not even Christmas. It's confusing. This could easily be a cult, and that's the first step in messing with my head on the way to conversion.

"Everyone, I'd like you to meet Nick," says Keith. "Nick, this is everyone."

I notice Keith is the only one *not* eating. He's too busy tapping his foot and introducing me, and it's one of those lazy introductions where no one really says anything back except a muffled noise.

"Well, that was a bit slack, Captain," says some sixty-year-old codger in the corner. "Why don't you just cover him in meat and throw the lad to the *dogs*?"

"Why don't you just go and fuck yourself, *Lunchmore*," Keith says, tapping his foot even harder.

The old codger scratches his forehead and takes a deep breath.

"Now, Keith," he says, standing up, "I've told you. Don't fuck with me, you arsehole or I'll stab you with this FORK."

He bangs his fist on the table, rattling all the cutlery and pots. Everyone jumps a little, then carries on eating quietly as if nothing had happened.

I dish up a few of the testicles with some gravy and rice.

"Meatballs," Keith says, lifting his head and smiling at me. It's the only smile that a speed addict can muster — one of great effort lasting only a couple of seconds.

"We're mostly atheists around here," says this young guy with scabs all over his face. It's a random thing to say since I didn't ask about anyone's religion. Still, there's a painting of either Jesus or Russell Brand on the wall.

"*Bullshit*" yells the codger Keith called Lunchmore. "*Don't* pack me into your assumed majority, you arrogant arsehole."

"No religion at the table, please," Keith says calmly. Then, he looks at me with his weak smile again. "Nor politics," he says, raising his eyebrows.

"Hi, Nick. My name is Brenda," says a woman at the end of the table. "I live next door."

I notice she's wearing fat wooden beads — possibly a rosary — over the brightest pink dress I've ever seen. It's close to the pink of a very healthy vagina. If we were on acid, our clothes would probably fuck.

"What's your story then?" Brenda says between mouthfuls of bollocks.

I pretend not to hear.

"Nick?" she says.

Now everyone's waiting for a bloody answer.

"Nah," I say.

"Excuse me?" she says, scrunching her face in confusion.

"Look," I say. "If this is one of those fucking meetings like *Narcotics Anonymous* or whatever, I'm not interested."

The paranoia hits instantly. There's bread on the table, and it's triggering me, so I pull out a Longbeach and light it up.

"No smoking at the table," says Lunchmore.

"*Shut it*, Lunchmore," Keith says.

"Fuck you, Keith, you *rat*," yells Lunchmore. He grabs a butter knife and leaps over the table toward Keith.

Lunchmore's right foot stomps in the testicle curry and sprays everyone with gravy. Next thing, he's on top of Keith, who has hold of Lunchmore's arm and the butter knife and is strangling him with the other arm. Purple-haired girl stands up and boots Lunchmore in the face a couple of times while Brenda comes up behind and sticks an injection into Lunchmore's arse.

"Take him down," Keith says, and the scabby fellow and Brenda pull the now drowsy Lunchmore out of the room.

"Sorry about that," Keith says to me.

"Fine by me," I tell him. "Even the gaff is quieter than this at dinnertime — usually."

❖

I'm sitting on the back step smoking Longbeach in the humid night air. I look down at my purple cock-head shirt, now splattered with red gravy, and I wonder what fucking madhouse I've gotten myself into.

Purplehead comes out and sits next to me on the step. She's beautiful, I think. It's hard to tell as it's been a while since I've seen a real-life woman.

She puts a ciggy in her mouth, and I light it for her with the lighter Keith gave me. I'm fucking King Arthur in my chivalry.

She takes a long drag, exhaling slowly. We watch the blue smoke disappear over the neighbour's fence and listen to the crickets for a few seconds.

"He's alright, you know. He's not really crazy," she says.

"Who, Keith?" I say.

She laughs.

"No, Lunchmore. He's not even really a Christian. He's just had a hard past."

I don't even know what that means.

"Trauma," she says.

"Don't we all have trauma?" I say. "It's not an excuse to attack people with knives, is it?"

Crickets.

"Do you want me to wank you off?" she says suddenly.

"What?" I say.

It's not that I didn't hear. It's just — *what?*

"Just that you've been in prison for a while, yeah?" she says.

She's right. I *have* been in prison, and yes. The answer is yes to everything. I'm nodding, and she starts undoing my belt.

"Not here, though, right?" I say, doing my belt back up.

"Why not?"

I mull it over for a second.

"I just don't wanna get my cock bitten by mosquitos," I say.

It's just a front. This isn't about mosquitos. It's that I just got here, and I don't want to be seen getting wanked off by the nympho. It's all a bit cliche.

She laughs like a hyena *again*, slaps me hard in the face *again* and fucks off inside.

I wonder if I said that last bit out loud. Sometimes that happens.

The crickets are laughing at me — those *pricks*.

Keith comes out and sits on the step next to me.

"I see you met Astrid then?" he says, pointing at the pink hand mark on my cheek.

"You're not gonna offer to wank me off, too, are you?" I ask him.

"Nah, but I made trifle if ya want some?"

The word trifle makes me think of the noseless guy with puke on his chin, and that makes me think of not being able to stop my thoughts, which makes me start to panic again.

I'm about to jump up when Keith says,

"9 am tomorrow, you free?"

"What for?"

"Soup Kitchen, Pal. It's part of the conditions of me keeping yer here. Nine till two pm two days — all I ask."

It's fine by me. It's something to do. I'd rather keep busy making soup than sit around with these damn thoughts, so I nod without saying anything.

"Good lad," he says, slapping me on the back and heading back inside.

Breaking Bread

I woke up nine times last night.

I know that because I kept a tally in the gaff, and it became a habit. The most it happened in there was seventeen and the average four to five. So, this was a big night. I can't get used to the freedom. I'm frozen by the liberty. Or maybe it was all the salt in that fucking testicle curry last night.

Breakfast is at 8 am. It's another serve-yourself buffet job. No testicles this time but bacon, eggs, cornflakes, milk, that kind of thing. Bacon is like Rohypnol to me. Feed me a couple o' rashers, and I'm anybody's. Cornflakes, on the other hand, taste too spicy — not like a vindaloo, more like someone has put pepper on them or laced them with tobacco powder — not that anyone would — not at fifty bucks a pack anyway. Coffee is a safe enough option. It's good percolator shit — weakish and unlikely to trigger a panic attack. It would be nice with a slug of Irish, but there ain't none of that shit here. This is the house of God, I think, or Manson. I haven't quite worked it out yet.

◆

It's 8.53 when I get to the House of Soup. Looks like a group of dodgy-looking fucks smoking — nothing virtuous about this place, and possibly a front for a drug operation.

I'm standing out the back, hitting a Longbeach, when Purplehead turns up.

"Better hope there's no Swiss cheese on the menu today, Conrad. Bring yer scissors?"

I don't know what the fuck she is saying. And I don't know what to say back. How does she know my surname? It's twenty-four hours since we met, and she's slapped me *twice* and offered to wank me off *once*.

I don't say anything but keep sucking on my Longbeach.

"Yer better hope they don't put yer on croutons," she says.

Croutons are bread. I hadn't even considered there might be bread involved. But, of course, soup goes with bread. *Fuck.* Anyway, why the fuck would she say that? Does she know about the bread thing?

"Why's that?" I ask.

"Because you'll be with The Count."

"The Count? Like Count Dracula?"

"Lunchmore," she says. "He got the nickname because he tends to bite people randomly."

"He won't bite me," I say. "I'm pretty confident of that."

My brain visualises beating the shit out of the old codger, and my heart starts racing.

I take a drag of the Longbeach, barely scraping past the orange filter. The smoke is hot. It tastes like fibreglass and burns my lungs, so I drop it and stomp on it.

"I'm fairly sure he will," she says, "that's all I'm saying. And if he does —"

"I thought that's all you were saying," I say, interrupting.

She stands up and gives me a look.

"Don't slap me," I say. "I'll fucking punch you back. I didn't have no daddy that told me never to hit women."

She leans into my face. For a second, I think she's gonna kiss me.

"You ever touch me," she says, "and I'll put a bullet in your skull, you *cunt.*"

I've been threatened a lot, and I know what's real.

She means it.

She is *Mike Jagger.*

❖

I'm not on croutons, and I'm relieved about that.

Not that I couldn't take the Count. I'm just starting again fresh, like a newborn baby into this world, innocent, pink and all that.

I'm on onions with the scab-faced guy. From what I can work out, Brenda is a supervisor. Keith is nowhere to be seen.

The scabby boy holds out a hand for the shaking. He introduces himself as Andrew. I nod and say,

"Nick."

This is the point where we would usually swap business cards. Mine would say,

Nick Conrad — Onion Cutter and Ex-Con

He shows me how to cut onions properly. At first, I think he's being an onion wanker, but I soon realise there's some clever horizontal cutting method. The kid's a fucking onion genius.

"So, what do you think of Purplehead?" I ask him.

"Who?"

"The girl with the purple hair?"

"Oh, that's Astrid. She's been at the house for about three weeks. From what I can gather, she's just come out of drug rehabilitation for MDMA. She also has a sex addiction."

My eyes are burning from onions. We should be wearing masks for this shit. It's like biological warfare.

"Why do you say she's got a sex addiction?" I ask. "Don't we all have sex addictions? If I had a choice of no sex or no food, I'd be a skinny prick like Keith. That's all I know."

"Well, she's had three guys over already, and that's against the rules," Andrew says.

This fucker doesn't know shit. He's repeating what Keith said to him.

"What's your story then?" I say, changing the subject. I don't really give a fuck, but talking is what you do when cutting onions since it keeps the thoughts at bay. Besides, I'm already crying my eyes out, so it's a good time to talk shit. If you get triggered, you can say it's the onions.

"Crystal meth mostly," he says.

You don't often hear addicts refer to their drugs so formally. Most citizens in methworld I know call it *Shards* or *Ice* or similar. Not that I'm a drug guy. Never have been much. I dabbled a bit in my twenties, but once I discovered capitalism, there was no need. The rush of making money was all *I* needed.

Fuck, I'm a cliche. Tie me to the stake already.

Andrew isn't a typical addict. He's intelligent and geeky. He tells me it started when he used drugs to stay up programming all night.

I ask him what his programming language is. I don't know why I'm asking since I know nothing about it. I don't even think that's the right way to ask.

He says something about a python, making me think of Arsehole Taylor's peach python in my intestine. I feel sick and get vertigo, but this is a good place for it, chopping the onions. I seem fucked up by the onions, but I've got cock up the arse trauma. I need to sit down.

He's still ranting on about some shit.

"Will you excuse me, Andrew?" I say, like we're in some corporate meeting rather than some scabby kitchen, and I go outside.

◆

I'm looking up at the sky now. It's blue. That's a good sign. If the sky is blue, things are relatively normal. It's something to hold onto — almost a *fact*, you could say.

My throat's dry as fuck from onions and Longbeach, and I'm alone again. The trouble with anxiety is you want to be alone, but when you are alone, you're not really alone. It's you and your thoughts. And those damn crickets. And none of them ever seem to shut the fuck up.

Think about the blue sky. It's blue. It's normal. *Don't* think about croutons. *Don't* think about croutons.

"You alright, Conrad?" says Purplehead, appearing on the steps next to me. No slaps, no wanking, just empathy.

The automatic response is a swift *yep*, and I want to follow it up with an apology for being a prick, but my mouth and throat are in the wrong shape. A quiver comes from deep in my stomach, and I burst out crying like a fanny instead.

She puts her arms around me. That's meant to stop it, but it gets worse.

Now I'm wailing like one of those dramatic bellends you see, and I can't stop it. This is just embarrassing. I want to tell her it's not me. My body is acting of its own accord. It's like an out-of-body experience.

"It's the fucking onions," I blurt out in an unnaturally loud voice.

She'll never believe me. Onions make your eyes water. They don't make you wail like a psycho. She doesn't laugh. She just keeps holding me. Then she hands me a rough napkin, and I wipe snot and crap from my face. I nod at her to say thanks and mumble about how I should go back inside because Andrew would have finished the rest of the onions by now.

The truth is, I need to stop this wailing, and that means getting away from her.

❖

"Sorry, Andrew," I say, shaking my head. "I know I'm not making the best impression on my first day."

I'm not sorry. This isn't a real job. It's slave labour.

"Fine, Mate," he says. "We're on croutons now anyway."

I'm okay with it, I think.

"I thought the Count was always on Croutons?" I say with an elevated heart rate, hoping Andrew has made a mistake.

"Don't let him hear you call him that," he says. "He'll bloody stab you. Anyway, he has an appointment today, so *we're* doing the croutons. I'll show you. It's easy, don't worry."

This fucker thinks I'm worried about being unable to under-stand the complex science of making crunchy bread pieces. I want to tell him he's a naïve prick. I want to punch him in the head for belittling my situation.

Deep breath.

It's not his fault. He has no idea about my shit. It wouldn't be *justice*. So, I divert my aggression to fantasising about taking the knife from that vampire Lunchmore and shoving it up his undead arsehole instead.

I like thinking about croutons. There's nothing in croutons to panic about. As Andrew taught me, we take yesterday's soup bread and tear it into pieces approximately the size and shape of 'a gram of weed'. I'm not a weed smoker, but from memory, it's just under the size of my left testicle, and having a size to work with makes it methodical, which distracts me from the fact that it's bread.

I watch him a few times. Then we get into it. I rip up the bread, and he adds olive oil, salt, and some Italian herbs and chucks them onto a tray. And the smell reminds me of the first time I smoked weed in a tent in my mate's backyard.

By the age of thirteen, two things were refined for me — my ability to play the piano and my knowledge of European cuisine. I remarked at the time how weed smelled unusually like dried oregano. We considered it a fact since we had nothing to compare it to. No one tells you that weed *actually* smells like a blend of sweaty armpits and cat piss.

Andrew rubs the croutons around so they soak up all the oil and the other shit. It smells decent, and I feel hungry for the first time since I got out. The only thing that puts me off is the possibility of

Scabby Andrew's scabs dropping in the croutons. But, fuck it. Protein is protein.

This process goes on for half an hour. I'm surprised at how many croutons we are making.

Andrew tells me *they* love the croutons. By *they*, I think he means the soup kitchen's clients. Who are they? The peasants of the modern world? Homeless? Junkies? Cheap fuckers who don't wanna buy their own food?

He tells me that we're the best soup kitchen around. I don't know what the fuck he means by that. The way he's talking, I expect Ramsay to walk out any moment and twat someone for serving raw scallops.

I wonder what competitor soup kitchens look like. Maybe I could go and work for them. Maybe I could work undercover and —

I realise that I'm smiling for the second time in a week. The first was with Astrid on the steps. It's an unusual feeling, accompanied by something like shame. I'm ashamed of smiling.

We stick the croutons in the oven at intervals so there are always fresh ones when the clients start filing through.

"Taste this," Andrew says after the first batch comes out.

"It's fucking hot," I mutter with a gobful of molten croutons blistering the top of my mouth.

"You *prick*," I say, grabbing Andrew's shirt. Then I let go and apologise immediately.

Apart from the temperature, he is right. They are good. I could just eat a plate of those. Fuck the soup.

We get to eat before the clients arrive. I sit next to Andrew, and Purplehead joins us opposite. It's comfortable. You don't have to watch your back in this place, and the soup is good too. For a minute, I feel mildly relaxed.

"I'm Astrid, by the way," Astrid says.

I can feel her pitying me, and you probably expect me to say something like, *I don't need your pity, Ma'am*. But fuck it. I could go some good old-fashioned pity. I've still got tear-stained cheeks from onions and psychotic wailing. I'm ashamed of the wailing, but I know the shame isn't real. My mind has been cooked by prison, and my wife getting fucked up by a truck. But it's not *just* that. There were *years* building up to it. Cheating on my wife with the Excel spreadsheet for years never helped. And my dog. *Fuck.*

My eyes are filling up again, so I stand up and walk out. I have to. I can't wail in front of everyone. Crying into soup is such a cliche.

I can't believe I'm one of those people who cry all the time now. I used to know people like me and think they were such fannies. That's part of the shame, I guess. It's me from the past looking at me in the future and calling me a fanny. I receive the message as shame, that's all.

I suppose it's some kind of karma. That's what that Zen teacher in prison would say. He told us that we *all* have to face up to our past. It's why I didn't fuck Scabby Andrew up for burning me with the croutons. I'm starting again fresh. I'm like a newborn baby in this world, innocent and, well, you know how it goes.

I'm sitting on the back step *again*. Fortunately, I can't hear those prick crickets because some exhaust fan is busy sucking the stench of vegetables and misery out of the soup kitchen.

These Longbeach are starting to taste like cheap cigarettes. I have to buy some better ones when I get some money.

Money — I'll need some at some point. Still, there are benefits to poverty. It keeps you out of trouble, for one.

Keith is taking me to get a phone tomorrow — something cheap, I imagine. It's the peak of my social calendar, besides this soup kitchen.

I've got no friends left. Who wants to hang around with a guy who assaults waiters for bringing out the wrong knife? *Nobody*, that's who.

I'm not saying what I did was right, by the way. I'm also not making excuses because I was grieving. I'm saying that just because I beat the guy up doesn't make him right to bring me a butter knife to cut sourdough. Maybe that's a dangerous way to think, but isn't there a right and wrong way to do things? Aside from deodorant, there has to be more that separates us from the animals, doesn't there? Would Ramsay be happy with a butter knife for sourdough? I doubt it. He would have a go at the waiter too. Maybe he wouldn't put him in hospital, but —

Fuck. I need to calm down. I'm getting angry again.

Astrid sits on the step next to me and hands me soup. I put out the cheap Longbeach and start slurping instead.

The purple-headed one digs into her pocket and pulls out a fistful of croutons, chucking them into my soup. A couple of the herb bits look blue now. That's probably fluff from her pocket, so I eat them anyway. Then I freak out. She is a druggie. What if there were traces of some shit in her pocket, and I've just eaten them. I won't find out for a good twenty minutes at least. What if there was *acid* in her pocket? FUCK. I'm not *ready* for an acid trip.

"Calm down," she says. "There's nothing in my pockets, you idiot." Then she keeps eating as if nothing unusual had just gone down.

I stare at her for a good ten seconds and wonder if it was part of my *own* internal dialogue but in *her* voice. Is she psychic? Surely she can't be because that stuff isn't real. No one can be psychic. There must be an explanation. Does that mean she heard my shit this whole time? Is she listening right now?

"Yeah, I'm listening," she says. "And may I just say you are one fucked up individual?"

It takes me another four seconds to realise that my worldview just split right open.

"Thanks," I mumble mindlessly while simultaneously dropping my soup bowl, which shatters on the sticky concrete.

I stare at it for a moment, and without looking at her, the words, *Do you want to fuck?* come into my head.

How embarrassing. This is fucked. She can hear *everything*.

The panic kicks in.

People think panic always relates to an object, but it doesn't. Panic becomes its own object. It winds itself up in itself, and you panic about panicking, and somewhere in there, it turns to terror.

"Sorry," she says, seeing me struggle like a doomed mouse just dropped into a snake pit. "I shouldn't have told you. No one else knows here, so keep it to yourself, eh?"

Her casual manner reins my terror in a little. I like it when she talks. I'm not thinking when I'm listening, so I can't embarrass myself.

It's interesting that when I'm listening or speaking, I'm not thinking. Does that mean listening and speaking are forms of meditation? Maybe I can talk and listen non-stop and be free of these terrifying thoughts?

What would the Zen Teacher say about that? I can't remember his name. Was it Zorro or Pancho or something?

"Good point," Astrid says. "Speaking and listening in isolation can be used as meditation objects if someone has concentration."

I stare at her again, wondering if this is it now. Is this the reality with this girl? Will she converse with my thoughts as if I'm saying them out loud?

"Sorry, Nick," she says again.

I remember that she can hear everything. I can't believe how easy it is to forget that.

I return to the present and try to think of something to say. I'm about to ask her how long she has been psychic as if we are on some new age date, but I don't get a chance.

"You'd better clean that up," she says, standing up and walking off.

I look down at the soup. Is it a symbol like the bird on the cow's back? Is the bowl my worldview and the soup all the conceptual shit I held around people's thoughts being private? Or is it just porcelain and vegetable soup on the floor — a mixed blessing for the ants? For some, a tsunami of thick orange matter, certain death. For others, a life-giving feast.

Astrid seems like a mixed blessing, but suddenly she doesn't seem so crazy or such a nympho.

"Serving time," Scabby Andrew says, popping his scabby head out.

I see clients arriving, and I wonder what the fuck is in that soup. Peyote? I should warn them.

Attention, homeless motherfuckers. Don't eat the soup unless you want your worldview shattered.

It doesn't matter anyway. They probably don't give a fuck. They are probably too busy trying to stay alive.

Service With A Frown

I'm on crouton service, lined up next to the other servers like an ugly school dinner lady.

The losers of society file past with their bowls of soup, but I'm shocked by how normal most of them look. I expected crackheads dressed in blankets for the most part, but these are ordinary people — quite a few families.

I've got an energy rush from those three mouthfuls of peyote soup, and now I want to talk to the citizens. I want to ask them why they are here. One woman comes past with three young kids. The kids look happy. She seems tired with great bin liners under her eyes. I'm wondering where the dad is. Maybe there isn't one. Maybe it's one of those post-nuclear homeless families or whatever.

I look down the line at Astrid, who is busy schlopping the soup into people's bowls and smiling like Oprah. *You* get some soup, and *you* get some soup. *Everybody* gets — I know she can hear me. I'm waiting for the romantic smile, but she doesn't even look.

I think about the noseless guy at the station. I want to give him some croutons and tell him I'm sorry for telling him to fuck off. Anyone could end up *sans nez*. I want to ask him where the fuck his nose is. I heard about those bankers losing their noses after doing too much cocaine, and I wonder if he is one of those. You can't tell once the downfall is complete. Look at me — ex-successful investor turned ex-con turned onion cutter, now crouton consultant. Can that fit on a business card? I might need to get double-sided.

"Can I get some croutons, Young Man?" says this old woman with skin flaking like an inflamed red croissant.

I'm filling up. I feel a wail coming on. I'm just staring at her, and she's just holding out her soup bowl. *Fuck.*

Astrid appears next to me and grabs my scoop. She shoves croutons into the woman's bowl, who mutters her thanks and shuffles along.

"Go take a break," Astrid says coldly. I feel like I'm letting her down. But why? This isn't her soup kitchen. Why do I feel this? She isn't my wife or my dog, or my boss.

I find myself on the step out the back for the fourth time today, but I don't light up a Longbeach. There's eight left from forty, and I don't have any money for more. Besides, I'm dehydrated, and my throat is worse than ever.

"Have you tried drinking water?" Astrid says, sitting next to me.

I haven't touched a drop all day. But it's good advice. Still, I'm sixty per cent water. Why don't I just drink mys —

I look her in the face — her pasty white beautiful face.

"I know why you slapped me," I say.

"Oh yeah?"

"Yeah. Because you heard my thoughts, and they were bad."

She smiles and looks up at the sky.

"Well, besides calling me the pastiest you'd ever seen, which I think is a bit of a stretch, you kept saying I'm a nympho, and I'm not."

I'm happy but disappointed. Does that mean she *isn't* going to wank me off?

She shakes her head, tuts and stands up, but I grab her arm.

"Astrid, wait." It's the first time I've used her name. "It's not me. It's my thoughts. I can't control them."

She sits back down and pouts at me.

"Didn't you meditate with that Zen teacher Akasuki in prison?"

She knows *everything*. She even knows his name. Not even I knew that.

"I tried," I say, "but I'm not sure he was the best teacher. I was also not in the best place getting —"

"Yep, I'm sorry to hear about that," she interrupts.

Fuck. She knows *everything.*

We sit in awkward silence for a few seconds.

"Maybe we can do a session some time? I can show you how it's done," she says.

I feel a rush of endorphins and get a lump in my throat. It's the pre-wail territory, but somehow, I get a grip and cry softly instead.

"I'd like that," I say. The fucking tears — I'm *broken.*

"Just to be clear," she says, "I was talking about meditating, not wanking you off."

I make a physical laughing noise. I haven't done that in a long time.

❖

So, this guy's name is Akasuki. It's distinctly Japanese, but the man is whiter than my foreskin. He is so white that his name is probably John, Peter, or some other good Christian name.

At the start of the session, he told us that Akasuki means *good friend* or some shit, but no one here cares.

I wish I could say this was one of those prison meditation sessions like in those documentaries where everyone behaves, and their lives are changed by it, but it's not like that. You've got to be ready for this kind of crap. If it was a matter of just shifting anger, no problem. But these guys aren't just angry. They are downright fucked up.

Akasuki is talking about how our innate Buddha is like a calm ocean, and the waves of emotions are like its waves. But he hasn't accounted for the weather, the stars, the sun, the moon, and infinite time and space. The trauma of these fuckers in Parisian night suits is as deep and vast as the sky.

Besides, this prick gets to leave at the end of the day. How am I supposed to find my Buddha mind when there's a good chance one of these other Buddhas might run me through with a shiv made from a damn toothbrush?

That would be appropriate for my life — death by toothbrush — symbol of a life lived worrying about how shitty your breath smells. Now *there's* a sermon. I should tell Akasuki about this. It's got to be better than the crap he is spewing at us.

Is it even called a sermon, or is that too Christian? It's probably something in Japanese. Maybe this whole thing is what they call an insight. That's what happens in meditation. Not that this is meditation. It's just a *memory*.

Now I'm remembering *her*. I remember her in a tropical bikini in our hotel room in Koh Samui, tying up her soft red hair in the bathroom, her tanned skin covered in grains of sand. I walk up behind her and kiss her back—the taste of soft salt skin. I push up against her and cup her stunning, firm breasts, cold and goose-bumped from the sea and —

Fuck. It's too hot under these covers. Sometimes you need to let your cock breathe, so I take it out and wank it in the fresh air with my eyes closed.

In my mind, I take off her bra. I slide my hand into her knickers and —

There's a loud knock, and my bedroom door swings wildly open within a millisecond.

"Oh fuck, My Man," Keith says, immediately turning away.

I need to explain to that fucker the logistics of knocking. I want to beat that prick to death with his Thermomix.

That was the first wank I had where I could get Arsehole Taylor's peach python out of my mind, and this prick just walked right in. Fuck. I should have locked the door. Why didn't I lock the door?

I don't like being locked in, okay?

◆

Breakfast is awkward. Keith is telling everyone that he walked in on me wanking. Everyone knows that grown men wank, but now they think it's all I do.

Nick Conrad — ex-con and morning wanker — that's me now. No point explaining to them that it was only my second wank in a week. They see a horny ex-con who has just gotten out of the gaff, even though it's not like that. I can see everyone's view of me has changed. They think I'm a pervert, but I'm not. I'm just traumatised.

Keith insists on taking me out to coffee to apologise. I accept, but not because I forgive him for busting me at my most vulnerable or for telling everyone, but because I know he has Longbeach. I don't, and I'm going to smoke his because he fucking owes me, that prick.

◆

I don't know why I agreed to this. There's an unusually high amount of well-built, short-haired white men in this coffee shop, and I wonder if this is a setup — either that or a golf convention, but golfers wear hats, don't they? It has to be a setup.

I served my time logistically rather than spiritually. Paranoia like this doesn't just go away. You have to work at it. That's what Akasuki said. He was right. You can almost taste it like gravy, but not nice gravy. It's rotting human flesh gravy with too much seasoning. It's the type of gravy Gordon Ramsay might crack the shits over, metaphysically speaking.

Keith has been talking for a while, but I haven't heard him. He strikes me as the sort of guy that doesn't notice when people aren't listening to him. Every time I tune back in from my paranoia, there's a different topic.

At one stage, he's saying something about the Afghanistan war or Afghani hash or something. I get soundbites about *druggies* and *sex addicts* and which shop sells the cheapest *johnnies,* whatever they are. Only joking. I know what Johnnies are.

"So look, probably the best choice is either Aldi or that newsagent on that corner run by the man who fackin stares at ya like he's gonna chase ya down and fack ya," he says.

This coffee is weak as piss, and the milk's a bit too creamy. That's all I need. Surrounded by milky, undercover cops, and these fuckers serve me milky coffee because they're undercover too. Everyone in this place is undercover. They want me to flip out at them so they can arrest me.

"So the soup kitchen is gonna shut down," he says.

Why the fuck is he telling me that?

"Oh yeah?"

"Yep. Running costs all piled up, Pal."

He looks like one of those thin dogs or ferrets after a bath, and it makes me want to punch him in the face. I also think he's about to ask me for an investment, but I know that's just my projected paranoia from being in that sphere of confusion known as the financial world. I've been bumming ciggies off this guy all week. Surely he knows I'm skint.

And yeah, now you're thinking I can't be much of a financial wizard. And you're right. But that's what happens when you're addicted to the game. You mortgage everything to the eyeballs. You risk it all to make more and more until one day, you can't pay your loans for whatever reason, and the whole thing goes tits up.

"I've got two dollars and sixteen cents," I tell him. "You can have all my money for fifteen per cent of the business."

He looks at me like I took a shit in his jacuzzi.

Somehow he falls into a biography of his life, and I reach for his Longbeach with a raise of my eyebrows. He subtly nods my approval, mentions Afghanistan again, then tells me about the minor hit he had called 'Poop Emergency' or some shit. He reckons it was a hit in Brazil and that they knew him as the Brazilian Hasselhoff. Now he's telling me how he got right into the coke on the back of the success but had enough royalties left to open the soup kitchen. If he's a liar, he's a damn good one.

"So look, Son," he says, "I know you ain't got no dosh, but they did tell me about yer background. Said you used to raise capital or something."

So he *isn't* after my money. He wants my free labour, and I want to explain that all my mental resources are accounted for in just about holding my shit together. But I don't. I nod and listen, and then I let him down gently.

"Look, Keith, Man. I appreciate everything you're doing for me, but I'm not ready to get back into the business world. I've been through a lot, and to be honest, I just need to think about getting a job so I don't steal all of your cigarettes."

He tells me I can have a whole carton of Longbeach if I agree. But I've been here before. It's like selling your winky for a half-bag of schmuck. The work involved would be too much—thirty grand in a month with zero contacts, assets or capital. I could do it, but it's just so much energy.

"Come on, Pal," he says. "We got the kitchen, the tools. We got a good van."

It's not a good van. I've seen it. It's a piece of shit, old Townace. Still, there are a lot of things you can do with a shit van. Making money isn't hard. Not letting money change you — *that's* the real challenge.

A waiter appears from nowhere.

"Can I get you any more coffee, sandwiches, pastries, or anything?"

Keith orders another damn skinny cappuccino.

I shake my head. I'm fine, but I notice the waiter is wearing a T-shirt that says, *Always shoot for the moon.*

I don't know what the fuck that means. Akasuki might know. He would give me some lame interpretation or read some Kungfucius or something:

> *The Wise Man always chases the moon.*
> *But at dawn, he will fish instead.*
> *Knowing the fish and the moon to be one*
> *He will live like a carrot in a fairground.*

Or whatever.

It could mean anything. *Always shoot for the moon.* Could be a pro-anal sex t-shirt.

"Come on, Son," Keith yells. "Help me, R2D2. You're my only hope."

All the milky cops turn around to look at us while Keith stares at me, waiting for a response. It's a fairly aggressive closing technique, and I have to respect him for that. But it's not about him. It's about me, and I don't have the energy.

"Stop hassling me, Keith, would you?" I say, instantly regretting the aggressive energy behind it.

I lower my tone.

"Look, you've been great to me, Man, and you do great work, and if this were six months from now, I'd be fundraising to turn you into a soup conglomerate."

"Cheers, Pal, but that's not the point here," he says. "Fack the corporate world. I think you'll have to get your shit together in less than six months, Pal. It's not like I have a deadline, but traditionally, tenants pay board of a hundred a week."

The bastard is turning dirty on me, pulling out the board card from nowhere. First, it's a hundred, then two. Before yer know it, you're paying rent.

"Why don't ya start by getting the dole?" Keith asks.

Fuck that. I'm not there yet. I just need to weather this storm until my mind calms down a bit. If I need to find a hundred for Keith, that's like a day a week washing dishes or holding up one of the stop signs, although those sign holders all seem to be hot chicks these days. Maybe I could get a blonde wig and some fake titties.

"I'm fine," I tell him.

I feel irritated and very paranoid about all these undercover cops around.

"I need to go," I tell him. "Do you mind if I take a few ciggies, Keith?"

"Nah, Pal. Just leave me two, and ya can take the pack."

I think Keith is alright, and it makes me realise that maybe I judge people on what stuff they give me. Is that what Akasuki would call an insight? Anyway, I like this bastard, but I'm still not doing his damn charity project.

"Thanks, Keith," I say, standing up and subtly watching all the undercover cops not even flinch but keep talking and drinking coffee. *Damn*, they're *good*.

I walk off to leave but turn at the last minute for some reason.

"Keith," I say.

"Yeah, Pal?" he says, looking at me hopefully through eyes of greasy kindness.

"You're alright," I say.

I instantly regret saying it. It feels like one of those sleazy seventies sitcoms where I jump up and freeze mid-air. The thought almost triggers an instant panic attack, but I catch it at the last second. Instead, I scowl and leave the place.

The Therapist

I always hated the idea of therapy. I always thought it was for weak people who didn't have their shit together. Maybe it is, but now I'm just one of them.

The reception at this place is lovely. It has polished wooden walls — wait — who has wooden walls? That's not normal. I feel the anxiety rushing on already — lousy timing to be here. Incidents and circumstances are just the inside men. They leave the shoe in the fire door after hours so anxiety can come in like Hudson Hawk and steal your courage.

This is where Akasuki would say something like *fear is the guardian of immortality* or some shit. He'd get me to imagine myself looking eye-to eye with the guardian armed with the sword of courage, but I can't just yet — next time. For now, I'll collapse emotionally and act weird as usual.

"Can I help you?" the receptionist says. She's wearing this fabulous burgundy dress with those pointy Mad Men secretary spectacles and the voice of a schoolteacher who wants to bend me over and spank me with a chopping board — a strange beauty in her.

I focus on her charisma, and I can act semi-normally.

"Hi, I'm Nicholas Conrad. I'm here to see —"

"Ah, yes. Thanks, Nicholas."

Smack, smack, *ooh.*

"He'll be with you shortly. Please take a seat."

Now, if I were a confident American, I'd say something like,

"Say, would you like to get dinner sometime?" and she would say,

"Sure, here's my number."

But I'm not, so I don't. I sit down instead. The wooden walls don't bother me too much anymore. I'm too busy looking at her burgundy beauty through the corner of my eye like a creeper.

The couch is that sexy brown leather like it belongs in a rich person's library rather than a psychologist's reception. And, damn, it's comfortable. There's sparkling water in glass bottles that probably comes from some underground lake in Monaco and heavy crystal glasses that you could knock a nail in with. This place isn't for ex-cons turned onion cutters. It's for rich bastards who drive European cars and have wallets made from albino giraffe leather. I might have come here back in the day if I'd had any desire to work on myself. Now it's a state-funded thing, so I'd expected some dirty white room somewhere, but I'm fine with this.

I flip over a glass and pour the glamorous soda. It's fizzing like money. I sit back down and take a mouthful. It tastes like champagne.

The door opens quickly, and a serious-looking man appears.

"Nicholas," he says, looking straight at me from the other side of the room.

Surely for the huge hourly fee, the therapist should come and greet you with a handshake. Not that I'm paying for it myself. Maybe he's forced to take various state-funded clients every month. Maybe he doesn't want me here, but he's paying back some debt to the government.

I take one last slug of the fancy fizz, nod at the receptionist, and she nods back with a reassuring smile but mildly concerned eyes. I might ask her out on the way back. Yes, I'll ask her out in the future. I'm comfortable with that. *Leave it in the future.*

I close the door behind me.

The room stinks like the spunk of a thousand millionaires. The view is unbelievable.

"This room is really —"

"Sit down," the therapist commands. He's a rude prick, but I'm fine with it. The more he barks orders at me, the more I don't have to think.

The decor is also a little seventies whorehouse, like a high-end version of the halfway house with fancy tarts rather than ghostly skanks. There's no trace of mince and potato flange here, just a supreme walnut coffee table with a beautiful crystal ashtray in the middle. Thankfully I came armed with Keith's Longbeach.

I pull out the packet and hold it up to him as if to say, *may I?*

"Please, go ahead," he says. There's a slight chance I might enjoy therapy.

I lie back on the couch. That's what's supposed to happen, I think. That's how this always goes in the movies.

"How have you been?" he says. I don't understand the question.

"Fine," I say. I don't know what I mean by that either.

"Why don't you start by telling me about yourself?" he says.

Damn it, now I have to speak to this guy. What do I even say? I'm no storyteller. I'm not fucking Charles Dickens or whatever. Can't we sit here in silence?

I should say *something*. He's writing in his notepad. That's not a good sign. He must have spotted something in me already.

"Where to begin?" I say like I'm a billionaire yacht guy with a cigar in my mouth speaking to a pretty young thing at a party.

"I was a fair squash player at school,"

What? Who gives a fuck about squash, you twat? I'm sure he will shit his pants from the sheer impressiveness of that statement. What's next, Oliver Twist? Did you end up in a workhouse or a gang in London? No?

I don't know what else to say. I don't want to tell my story. I'm not ready.

"I don't want to tell my story. I'm not ready," I tell him.

He thinks for a minute, then taps his pen on his notebook.

"Well, just tell me *a* story," he says. "It doesn't have to be *yours*. Just *anything*."

Anything? What does he mean by that? This is the age of computers. No one tells stories anymore. Am I supposed to recite Gulliver's Travels, Hamlet, The Matrix or some shit?

"How's the halfway house going?" he says. Maybe he already knows everything, and I won't have to fill in my life biography.

"Yeah, it's great," I say. Surely I can manage extra this time. This conversation could be going better.

"There's a girl there," I say. "Her name is Astrid. I think she's a nutter, but maybe I'm in love with her. She has purple hair, which is a bit cliche."

I sound like a stereotypical mad person.

"Why do you think the purple hair is cliche?"

He's got me there.

"Well, just because — well, I *don't*, I guess."

We pause. It's going well so far. I look out the window. It's a beautiful view of the city and the river here. It's the perfect place to be in therapy.

I've got a question for him.

"What do you think of the phrase, *always shoot for the moon*?" I ask.

He acts all taken aback like I asked about his sperm count.

"Well, it would depend on what context it was in," he says. "It could be a sporting reference, a spiritual one, or self-development. There could be a tremendous amount of meanings. Where did you hear it, Nicholas?"

I'm trying to remember where I heard it. I can't even remember if that was the phrase. Was it Akikaki who said it? Wait, was his name even Akikaki?

The fucking panic is here. This isn't good. I need to go. I need to get outside and — *wait* — is that *whiskey* I can smell? He keeps opening and closing the drawer.

"Are you drinking whiskey?" I ask. It's a bold question, and I want it to be true. But I've said it in an accusatory way.

"Yeah. Would you like one?" he says casually.

I never knew you could drink in therapy. That *could* be champagne in the reception too, just a young one. Sometimes they look like water, the newer ones. Old ones are deeper, more golden, and richer. My heart is racing.

"Yes, please," I say casually, like I hardly care. Is this standard therapy practice? Surely not. How would they go with the alcoholics? He pours me a generous half-crystal glass, and I take hold of it like

Excalibur and nod at him like he just returned my daughter from kidnappers.

"Cheers," he says.

I cheer back and drink a third of it. This is fine shit. Old whiskey is like old champagne. It's darker. That's what happens as we get older. We get darker, don't we? Is that an insight? No, it's just bullshit. That's excellent whiskey, though.

"That's excellent whiskey," I say, laughing.

I expect him to laugh back at me with a joyful face, and we can dance in a circle for a moment and sing some song to celebrate our bond and —

"Why don't you tell me about your wife," he says, taking a dump on our moment of happiness. It's a bit much. Let me enjoy my whiskey, for fuck's sake. Maybe I don't want to be here after all.

"Sorry, Nicholas," he says as if reading my thoughts. "That was too direct."

I suddenly remember Astrid's psychic ability and wonder if I should ask him how he feels about it. Then, I realise I don't know this man well enough. Maybe he could have me committed for being a mad bastard.

He lights up a cigarette.

"What kind of cigarette is that?" I ask, forgetting entirely about the Astrid thing.

"It's a *Marlboro*, Nicholas. Do you want one?"

I do want one. I stub out my throat-drying chemical-soaked Long-beach and reach for his outstretched Marlboro — *it's a more organic cigarette.*

I should get into advertising.

"I was obsessed with jingles when I was a kid," I say.

The Marlboro and whiskey have broken the ice.

"I memorised them all and sang them to my mum and dad. I drove them nuts with it. I thought about getting into advertising for a while."

He asks why I never pursued it.

"It would have suited me," I tell him. "I was a gift of the gab talker like no other — a real sharp-tongued lizard."

"Is that a song line?" he asks. It's not a song line. I just made it up.

"I just made it up," I tell him.

He likes that. This guy might be interesting.

"That's impressive," he says, but he isn't taking any notes. Surely that's a good sign. Surely he only writes down the bad shit. It could also be because his hands are full of Marlboro and whiskey.

"Funny you mention song lines," I say, "My mum always wanted me to be a songwriter. They had me classically trained in piano. I had friends who were songwriters, but they never made any money. So, I got into business instead."

I'm on a roll, and he seems to like my Ted talk. Why shouldn't he? I'm an interesting guy. I've had an interesting life.

"And where are your parents now?" he says.

This guy knows how to piss on your chips.

"*Dead*. They're both dead," I say, taking an enormous gulp of whiskey and staring out the window.

"Sorry to hear that, Nicholas," he says. "Would you excuse me a minute?"

He stands up and disappears into this hidden door in his office. What a rude bastard. Asks me about my parents and then fucks off into his secret bog. He must need a piss badly. Come to think of it, I did notice him jiggling around a bit.

That toilet must be soundproof. I mean, it *must* be unless he's just standing in there doing fuck all, not even breathing, which would be weird and pointless.

It's dead quiet until the toilet flushes. I heard *that*. It's not soundproof. He's just a quiet pisser. What could that mean? Poor prostate or something? Maybe he *couldn't* piss but was standing there trying, and he flushed to save face. Anyway, it doesn't matter.

"Sorry about that," he says, sitting in a chair closer to me. This is intimate, and it's weird because I feel a bit drunk and maybe a bit vulnerable — not sexually vulnerable, just emotionally.

At least I feel safe from the panic wolf.

I look at the clock and can't believe fifteen minutes have passed. They say time flies when you're getting your jollies. What has been said? Anything? Just a few words, I think. Is it possible to get paranoid from whiskey? Or it's the Marlboro. Maybe I'm allergic to Marlboro. Maybe I should have stuck to Longbeach. Oh well, it's in my blood now. You have to try and ride it and —

"Are you okay, Nicholas?" he asks.

I *think* I am. I think I'm holding on.

"Fine," I say.

"Is this the therapy?" I ask. I don't know why I'm labelling things. It's just something to say. Of course, it's the damn therapy. You've got everything you could ever wish for — a beautiful couch, a beautiful view, expensive whiskey, and Marlboro cigarettes. You're going places, Kid. We need to pull it together and try to enjoy these moments. Damn, do I feel crazier because I'm on the therapist's couch?

"Yes, this is therapy," he says. "It's better than the normal *tell me about your father* crap, right?"

He's talking about Freud, I'm pretty sure. He seems almost sexually turned on by his alternative methods. I think he thinks he's Robin Williams in Dead Poets Society. *Oh, Captain, my Captain.* He won't see me getting up on my fucking chair for him if that is what he's chasing. He's wasting his time.

I don't answer. I can't. I'm only mildly sure what he means.

"We have to move things along, or this shit might go on forever."

I realise I've said this last line out loud, not within the confines of my cranium, where it was supposed to remain until the end of time.

The guy smiles and takes a drag on his Marlboro.

"You were saying how you used to annoy your mother with your jingles," he says.

That's when I know it's me who is holding things up, not him. This guy is good. Why did I bring up the jingles, though?

"You mentioned you thought about getting into advertising and how you were a sharp-tongued lizard," he says.

Yes, I *did* mention that.

"I realised that Advertising took too long. You're at the mercy of time, and no one wants to be there. So I learned to trade. I made money at it, but I hated it. I wasn't patient enough and didn't have the stomach to be a scalper. It's watching the charts that gets you. It's the visual embodiment of capitalist heroin — the red and the green fighting for supremacy — wrestling and rolling all over the chart and breaking through walls like an old Kung Fu movie. Watching those charts is like betting. It's the watching I can't take. I realised I needed something I could control in real-time, so I decided enterprise was where it was at, and I started buying businesses. I would run a business for a while, improve it and sell it."

I've used those words a million times. They're drilled into my head for eternity. It's basically my LinkedIn profile word for word.

Is this what therapy is? Do you sit and listen to yourself harping on like an old ballbag, and eventually, you just say to yourself, *Oh, shut the fuck up. You sound like a cock,* and then you're therapised?

He's on his phone now, swiping one-handed and drinking whiskey. His cigarette is dangling from his mouth.

It's unorthodox. *Oh, Captain, my Captain.*

"Just looking at your record," he says.

At least he isn't on Tinder. Allegedly.

"What do you think you are going to do with yourself, Nicholas?"

It's a good question.

"I suppose I have to do *something* with myself. I can't sit around sipping whisky, smoking Marlboros staring out that window, living the good life, can I?"

Again, it's meant for the head, but it comes out as words. I'm waiting for his reaction now.

"You're a really interesting person," he says.

I used to know that. But as soon as he said it, I laughed at myself like a prick of an older sibling taunting the young one. I need to share this with the therapist.

"I used to know that," I say. "I used to have confidence in it. I could talk to anybody anywhere and feel right at home. But you become too confident in your life and believe you're in control. That's the mistake. Then something happens that just fucks you so profoundly. It's like getting hit with a sledgehammer, and you don't know if you'll ever recover. And it's like, *here's your new reality.* There's no one to strike a deal with or negotiate with. And I'm like, all this time, I'm doing all this to protect my family, and I can't protect them at all. There's *nothing* you can do. It's over."

I've got his full attention now, but I still don't want to talk about bread and waiters.

"Nicholas, facing new realities is one of the hardest things humans have to deal with. And as a therapist, I wish there was a way to explain it or frame it in a way that renders the pain irrelevant. But to this day, I have not found a way. I see you attended some meditation classes in prison."

"I did. His name was Akasuki. He was a Zen monk and a white guy. Not that *that* matters at all. But I feel like it needs to be mentioned to frame the relevance of the name and all that."

The therapist looks at me, tapping his pen on his notebook as if he's going over some pattern he learned at University. That's probably fake. He's probably thinking about how many calories are in the Greek salad he had for lunch or when the new season's pants will arrive.

"You speak with a certain degree of aggression toward the Zen teacher?" he says.

Is that a question or a statement? But yeah, he's right, and it's crazy. I didn't realise that myself until he just pointed it out.

"I suppose I do."

The therapist's silence means I'm supposed to keep talking now.

"Look," I say, "I'm all for people following their paths. And I'm not bothered that he's a Western person because I don't have the passion to give enough of a fuck. So I go off what he says and does. And to be honest, a lot of it was just sitting there."

He's nodding.

"And a lot of the stuff he said seemed either cliche, lame or — nah, they're the wrong words. It wasn't cliche or lame. It was just, let's say, *tepid*."

"Tepid?"

"Yeah, you know, *lukewarm*."

I still don't think that's an accurate translation of how I felt about it.

The therapist takes a plug of whiskey and lights another cigarette, offering me one too. Since I had that insight, we all know I like people because they give me things. So, of course, I take it and smoke with him. And, of course, I start to really like him.

I'm easily bought like a cheap hooker.

He's writing something in his notepad. Something was meaningful about what I just said. What was it I just said?

"Do you think you would have felt differently if his name was Simon?" he blurts out.

It's a good point, and I know the bloody answer.

"Yes, I think I would," I say. "I mean, that would be *authentic*, wouldn't it?"

Now he's nodding *and* writing. Surely *that* means something.

"And outside of prison, would you even go to a meditation class with a teacher called Simon?"

I see his point, but he's wrong. Before prison, I wouldn't have gone to a meditation class at all.

"So what is it, Doc?" I say.

He frowns and looks at the floor.

"What am I?" I continue. "A racist? An anarchist? A fundamentalist?"

"It's too early for diagnosis," he says. I'm sure he knew that I already knew that. I'm just a bit drunk.

"But, I'd say that maybe the Zen teacher affected you more than you think. Do you understand?"

I do understand. He's right. I'm always thinking about that Zen bastard.

"I do understand," I tell him.

"And let's not assume either that the Zen teachers were all kind, gentle people," he says.

We both laugh, but I don't know what is even funny. It's just the booze and the feeling that I don't want to disappoint him. It's *pathetic*.

Still, it's going better now. I feel relaxed in this guy's presence. He has won me over. What a cheap bastard I am. I hate myself.

He keeps talking, and I listen.

"And let's not assume that the symbolic beatings from a Zen master are limited to pigeonholing it to the classic physical violence or verbal abuse. People find ways to deal with *those* things. Forms of psychological torture are very high on the agenda. Don't you think it's interesting that we venerate such things as part of the spiritual path?"

This guy is interesting but too far down the road for me. I'm not up for a political or spiritual discussion. Honestly, I'd rather sit here, drink whiskey and say nothing. It helps. It really helps.

"Carpe Diem," I yell, opening my eyes suddenly. Something feels different. I've been asleep, but I don't know for how long.

The therapist is at his desk typing.

"What happened?" I ask him.

"You fell asleep," he says. "I thought you might need the rest, so I just left you, and I've been getting on with some other work."

"Thanks," I say like he did me a favour, but I can't help but think that was an expensive sleep.

He tells me to come back at the same time next week, and I shuffle out the door. I pass the empty receptionist's desk and scan the area for my burgundy secretary, but she isn't there.

It's one last disappointment of this strange outing.

The Grey

I'm not sure of the point of therapy. I felt pretty good before I crashed out, but now I've got a bit of a headache and a bit of depression, and I've got to leave my comfy couch by the window and return to these shitty streets.

The elevator opens, and I wander onto this corporate street in a whiskey haze. The problem with not drinking for a while is you don't just get drunk, you also get tired. And now it's pissing with rain, and I don't have an umbrella or anything. I can't say I care. I've got Keith's cock-head shirt on, and to be fair, it could use a wash.

The sky's gone grey, and it's going to storm like a bastard. Something has lifted, though. It could be the whiskey, but something else. That session was strange if I think back. In my memory I was in that office as a child. Well, not a child, probably more like a teenager. I don't know if therapy is *meant* to feel like that. The actual guy, well, it felt like he didn't give a flying fuck, but maybe he did. It's definitely one of the weirder things I've had to do — drink whiskey and smoke during therapy. Don't you usually go to therapy to get rid of those things?

There's a young woman in a white dress running in the rain. Her tits are bouncing up and down. I realise I haven't seen that kind of thing for some time, and it turns me on. At the same time, I feel some bizarre shame. I have to consider if it's because Keith, that greasy prick, walked in on me having a wank. If I were still in that bastard therapist's office, I'd ask him, and he would tell me it's a lot deeper than that. Who needs a therapist? I already know what's happening. As I said, that was an expensive sleep I had up there.

What am I doing? I'm standing outside this bank watching the white tits disappear up the street, and I'm getting pissed on by God's golden shower.

I've got a semi-hard-on and about nineteen bucks. If this were nineteen seventy-two, I'd be off to the brothel now to get my cock sucked, but it isn't. I doubt nineteen bucks will even buy you a copy of Playboy these days. Does Playboy even exist? Come to think of it, who would purchase porn these days when the internet is full of free shit?

Keith asked if I would be home for the usual chaotic dinner, and I said yes for some reason. Still, that gives me half an hour to play out whatever dangerous whiskey fantasy takes my pleasure.

Let me see now. I could rob someone — not a woman. And it can't be an old codger or a young bloke — maybe a fifty-year-old guy in a suit who still has some guts left in him to put up a fight. Maybe with a bit of luck, he might be packing a copy of the Sunday Times, which he rolls up and beats me to death with like Jason Bourne. That would be easy. But it's not Sunday, so it's unlikely.

Maybe I'll go and flash my cock to someone. Again, it can't be a woman. How about one of those Big Bird cab drivers? — and not for any sexual reason, but just to satisfy this whiskey urge.

That's it. I'll stick my balls on the hood of his car and spunk onto his windscreen, for God's sake. That should help this sickness, whatever it is. Maybe I'll live on the streets and make a habit of spunking on car windows. I'll become infamous like fucking Batman. I'll talk in a hoarse voice like I swallowed a cock ring, and I'll call myself *The Night Prawn*.

I wish I'd known my plans when the therapist asked. I would have told him precisely about The Night Prawn, right down to his pink lycra outfit with the big P on the front.

This shitty phone that Keith gave me is ringing, interrupting my creative surge. But I don't have any numbers. It must be a telemarketer or something.

"Hello."

"Nick, it's Astrid."

Fuck, I forgot she was clairvoyant again.

"Well, this is embarrassing," I say.

"Don't be embarrassed," she says, "I just wanted to say, as your attorney, I advise you not to ejaculate on taxis but just come home and eat some dinner. I'll give you that wank, too, if you aren't too much of a *cunt* about it."

She hangs up the phone immediately. There's nothing more to say. I abandon the Night Prawn project until another day. I straighten my cock-head shirt and head home to get wanked off by a girl instead.

I need that.

◆

It's six forty-five PM. I avoid the deadly bush and unlock the front door of this red-brick whorehouse once again. The smell of mince and potato flange hits me square in the nasal chakra, and I hear Lunchmore swearing from the kitchen. I can't handle this right now.

It's *fine*. Just think about the wank. Just think about the wank.

All the crazy bastards have gathered for dinner — the mad hatter and the silver paint sniffers and mercury heads.

There's a big plate on the table with bits of grey meat. Damn, food is disgusting.

I see Astrid from behind cutting some shit in the kitchen. I don't want to make mental sexual comments because I know she can hear everything, but I'm nervous about her wanking me off. No girl has been near my cock in a long time. It needs a damn makeover and could use a trim since the pubes are longer than the shaft.

I appreciate Astrid's direct nature. How else will I get wanked off? Am I meant to talk to a woman? And say what? I'm not one for classic chat-up lines. *Say, do you like bananas?*

Astrid bursts out laughing in the kitchen. People must think she's mental, always laughing to herself. It's no wonder they think she's nuts. *Fuck.* Now she's coming my way.

"Astrid," I say, nodding.

I brace myself for a slap in the face or a kick in the knackers. She does neither but kisses me on the lips and rubs my crotch with her hand. We're in the dining room, for God's sake. This isn't the place for the wank, surely — not with the grey meat watching.

"You think too much," she says.

She's right about that — especially now my thoughts aren't private. I wish I could stop them though I — *fuck*. I feel the hot and cold sensation again.

A damn panic attack is coming on. I consider hitting the streets for an evening jog, but she pulls me tight into her. She grabs my hand and slides it down the front of her knickers, and I calm down immediately. It's much more effective than a McDonald's paper bag.

"Breathe long and slow," she says, and I do what I'm told. She unzips my fly, gets my overly hairy pecker out, and wanks it slowly.

"Nicholas," says Lunchmore barging into the room. "Nice of you to join us."

I pull away from Astrid and sit down at the table quickly. I don't know why I care so much. Who cares if Lunchmore is in the room? I should just let her make me blow. I *need* that.

Keith and Brenda join us now with bowls of gravy and sprouts. They're talking about the damn soup kitchen, as always.

Astrid sits down next to me then everyone else sits down.

Brenda takes my plate and starts serving me sprouts.

"How many sprouts do you want, Nick?" she asks.

I want to give her a straight answer, but I can't because Astrid has my cock out under the table, and she's massaging it like a damn pastry chef.

"I'm not sure," I say, "You decide."

She gives me an odd look.

"Decisiveness is one of the keys to success in this world, Nicholas," says Lunchmore.

I want to tell him that I'm very decisive and that I decisively want everyone to stop focusing on me and serve their own damn sprouts. Astrid is the only one I want to focus on my sprouts right now.

Astrid giggles at that, and I would laugh too, only I'm concentrating on not levitating out of my seat.

"Fack off, Lunchmore. Who are you? Anthony Robbins?" says Keith.

Lunchmore mutters under his breath, but I'm close enough to hear.

"I'll slit your throat in your sleep, Captain," he whispers.

"Astrid, would you like meat, love?" says Brenda.

Astrid ignores her because she's looking straight at me intensely while I look straight ahead at the photo of Russell Brand on the wall. Forgive me Fath —

Astrid knocks her fork off the table.

"Please excuse me," she says, disappearing under the table. I think about the scene from Police Academy where the hooker is under the podium, and I burst out laughing. It's fine. Spontaneous laughter is perfectly acceptable in this house of sprouts.

"What about you, Nick? Would you like some meat?" Brenda asks.

"I don't give a fuck," I yell, grabbing the table for dear life. "Oh *fuck me*," I scream, "FUCK," banging the table with my fist.

"Are you okay, Nick?" Brenda says.

"Course he is," Keith says, grinning. "Astrid don't need no meat. She's already getting it and sprouts too, I imagine."

"*Help me*," I say to Lunchmore as I begin levitating out of my chair.

Astrid appears next to me again, and she's wanking me hard now — finishing strong. I look straight back at her now and grab her hair.

"Oh no, you two," Brenda says. "Not at the dinner table, *YOU TWO*."

I don't give a fuck anymore. I'm floating in the centre of the universe. I'm Major Tom. I'm Napoleon. I'm Homo eroticus troglodytes. I'm a motherfucking Tyrannosaurus Rex. I've *never* been wanked off like this before. She *must* be a nympho — the skills —it's just so damn — I remember she can hear me again and realise

I need to shut the fuck up and stop analysing it. I'll leave her an Amazon review later.

I pull her hair, and she pushes her right index finger under and up into my arsehole. The bliss soaks my whole being, and my perineum expands and contracts like the damn FTSE 100. I feel spunk spraying from my cock in quantities I never thought possible, and I dissolve completely into atoms.

When I come back, the Count has stood up.

"What the fuck? What the fuck?" he's saying.

"What the *fuck, Nicholas*?"

He's wearing summer shorts, and my spunk has coated his pasty white vampire legs.

I want to apologise, but I can't. My eyelids are heavy, and I might have to pass out.

The Count grabs a butter knife from the table and comes at me.

"I'll *kill* you," he screams, bearing his fangs and closing in.

At the last moment, Astrid lays out a great boot, and the Count takes it in the teeth. She gets behind him, and Keith and Brenda grab him from the front. They struggle to wrestle the old bastard to the ground. He is as strong as an Oxo cube.

"Just leave him," I say, feeling sorry for the old wombat shagger. Who am I to judge? I beat the shit out of a waiter for giving me the wrong knife. That waiter didn't even spunk on my legs.

Keith sticks the syringe into Lunchmore's left arse cheek, and they drag him out of the room as they do just about every night.

Brenda notices my look of empathy for the Count.

"Don't judge them too harshly for drugging him, love," she says as if I didn't just orgasm in front of her or spunk on a man's legs, or as if she didn't just observe that same man getting kicked in the teeth and dragged to the basement. "He goes off at something every night. If it weren't you ejaculating on his legs, it would have been something Keith said. You were just a vehicle for his violence tonight. Nobody wants to restrain him, but he would have bitten your nose off if we didn't. He is very dangerous, Nick. I hope you understand."

I don't even give a fuck that much. I'm thinking about the noseless guy and feeling terrible for the bastard. I wonder if everyone gave him that damn look I gave him — that look that says, *I want you out of my life.*

Then I think about Astrid and the feelings I'm developing for her. I know she's a meditator because she offered to teach me, but she also seems like a psychopath. I've watched her attack the Count twice. She's also physically attacked me several times and threatened to put a bullet in my skull. But I don't feel anxious or depressed at all. I still partly have the whiskey in my system and had forgotten the healing power of getting professionally sucked and wanked off.

I go to the bathroom and rinse off. Then I come back to the table, grab a sprout and hong down on it. It's crunchy, and I can't stand crunchy vegetables. I don't want to touch the grey meat, but the whiskey made me a bit hungry, so I shove down a couple more of the little green bastards.

Keith wheels in a giant whiteboard and writes on the top of it.

Soup kitchen funding ideas.

I already told the bastard I wanted nothing to do with it. Can't a man eat crunchy sprouts in peace?

He looks like a speed-addict team leader about to embark on a training session.

"So, guys, thank you for participating in today's brainstorming session."

Astrid appears again from the basement.

Did you agree to this? I ask her mentally. She sits down and cuts her meat without saying anything.

Hello? I say with my thoughts again. She's ignoring me. Maybe I imagined that she was clairvoyant. I don't know. I'm high off whiskey and spunking. Anything is possible.

For fuck's sake, Astrid, I —

"Talk to me like a *real* person, Nick," she barks at me across the table. That's one way to break the positive wave I was riding. She's good at kicking me in the dick. She puts her hand on top of mine and apologises. That's nice, at least.

Now Keith is ranting on about the costs of the soup kitchen and writing each one down. Brenda is taking notes, and Scabby Andrew is in the kitchen doing the dishes. I'm still trying to understand why everyone feels obliged. It's *his* soup kitchen and —

"You still don't get it, Nick, do you?" Astrid says out of the blue.

She's right about that. I don't get much at the moment. The anxiety is back because the whiskey is wearing off, and Astrid's bipolar approach isn't helping much. She takes her hand off my knee and physically moves her chair away.

Keith wants us to go around the room and each present an idea to make money for the soup kitchen. Scabby Andrew pops his head in and suggests a raffle. I have to stifle my scorn with a cough.

"Sure," I say, "a good raffle will make you at least a grand."

Now everyone is looking at me. I shouldn't have said anything. I'm unwittingly involved in this damn project. *Fuck it.*

"What you need to do," I say, "is cross whatever is popular with whatever skills you have."

Everyone looks at me like I'm a university professor. Keith has obviously told them about my background, and I don't like where this is going, but I've started now.

"For instance, Andrew has IT skills. Astrid is a meditator. Brenda is — well, Brenda makes a good cup of tea."

Brenda gives me the middle finger.

"Why don't you do an online meditation course of some kind?" I say. "I mean, that shit is popular these days, isn't it?" I'm just chucking stuff out there to get them off my back. And I'm thinking of Akasuki now. I believe his skills lay not in his actual meditation but in his networking ability. He probably got himself a Zen robe from eBay and responded to a tender to teach inmates. You only need to say the right things and sit in silence. It's not like anyone can see your inner experiences to note if you are genuine. It's not like —

"I'd say it would be easier to organise a real-life course," Andrew says, popping his head around the corner. "There's a fair bit of infrastructure to get together to do that kind of thing online. It's not necessarily hard, but it's the kind of thing where everything takes a long time to do."

He's right. And everyone is now discussing my idea. Now the cogs are turning. For a second, I'm back in the East counting coins like —

"Look, this isn't gonna happen," Astrid interrupts. "We're not starting a cult, for God's sake."

"I think a cult is a bit of a leap," I say. I'm subconsciously keen to get into an argument with her. "We're only talking about a meditation course, Astrid — maybe a week-long thing. I don't know. What do people pay for that kind of thing?"

"Look, I'm okay about teaching," she says. " I'm just not okay about teaching simply for the money, even for a good cause. There has to be a deeper layer than that. Why don't you idiots have a jumble sale or sponsor each other to shave your balls or something?"

I've been staring at her differently since the incident. The purple is fading slightly from her hair, and I notice how she looks for the first time. There's a tiny scar on her forehead and another one on the left of her nose. The nose scar is shaped like the South Island of New Zealand, and the head scar is like the North Island. Her eyes are grey-green like the ocean in between the two islands, and there's a tiny dot on the left one.

My American cousin had the same dot in his eye. He was eating one of those bloody corn dogs on sticks Americans love when an old man dropped his walking stick, and my cousin Chad leaned forward to pick it up for him and stabbed himself in the eye with his corn dog stick. Poor Chad was training to be a pilot at that time. It was a career-ending move. I told him that would teach him for trying to do the right thing. Now he's a financial manager in Minnesota.

"Mine is natural," Astrid says suddenly. I realise she's talking to me, and I have again forgotten about her ability to read my mind. I sounded like a real wanker there, as well.

"No, it was *sweet*, Nick," she says.

Keith has been mulling over something this whole time and has drawn some diagrams on the board, which I thought related to fundraising, but I now realise relates to the problems encountered when shaving a ballsack.

"What's the problem with starting a cult anyway?" I say suddenly, interrupting Keith's testicular Ted talk. "I mean, it's a very viable financial option these days. Rather than pay for courses, cult followers donate huge sums of money to their leader."

I know this because I watched this documentary once about this cult leader guy in prison. This guy had about a hundred Rolls-Royce cars. He lived like a damn emperor. And I don't know why people judge the authenticity of a spiritual teacher based on how much money they like to spend. I put that guy next to Akasuki, and I see a man not afraid to express his human madness fully. At least that guy was Indian — I think— and not some British plumber called Ted.

Then there's the sexual side of things. I never saw the Rolls Royce guy in a pair of speedos touching up his students like that weird yoga guy — not to say that didn't happen behind the scenes. Then again, who knows what Akasuki gets up to in his spare time? I doubt he would have had the guts to act up like that in a room full of inmates, even though a few might have enjoyed the attention and I don't —

"You're quite right," Astrid says to no one in particular, and I wonder if she's addressing me or Keith, the bullock-barber. "There's no way to tell the authenticity of a true spiritual teacher," she says. "Some are very humble, and some wild and extravagant."

She *was* talking about my stuff. I think about what the others must think about her random statements and laughter, and I realise that she trusted me with the knowledge that allows me to understand her while they all think she's a mad nympho. She gives me a look to warn me that she's going to kick me in the knackers.

The conversation about cults and meditation lasts about ten minutes while Scabby Andrew has been in the kitchen. He now emerges with 'hot chai' for everyone. It's made with milk, and there's a terrible brown skin on the top of it. It stinks like an Indian brothel and tastes like camel spunk.

"You're a fucking *racist*," Astrid says.

To them, it's another random statement, but I know what she means. I consider diving back into my Ted Talk about how racism is conditioned into me like Arsehole Taylor's spunk, but I have no time for that. I'm getting hooked on this idea of starting a cult to fundraise, and I realise I'm enjoying myself a bit.

Astrid shakes her head again and stands up. She grabs the magic marker off Keith and tells him to sit the fuck down.

"If we are going to do this," she says, "let's do it right. Nick, give me your shirt."

I don't know why she wants my shirt, but I can't say no. I undo the buttons of my beloved cock-head shirt and throw it at her. She uses it to wipe Keith's drawings off the board.

"That's *my* facking shirt," Keith says.

"Keith," says Astrid in her best schoolteacher voice. "Sit the fuck down. Do you want to save your soup kitchen or not?"

"Yes, Ma'am," he says, saluting like an army cadet.

Now I'm sitting there topless, and I can see Brenda checking me out in the corner of my eye. I feel her looking at my nipples, and I don't mind at all. The whiskey and the wank have triggered *something else* in me. She's not young. She's a little overweight. But there's an aggression in my desire. I want to go into her bedroom at night and *force* myself on her.

It's an unwholesome thought that could get dangerously out of control, and I think it might be born from wanting to balance myself from being the victim of the same. I *hate* myself for having it, but the more I try to push it away, the more it begins to control me.

I have to focus on Astrid, who appears not to be listening to me because she's busy planning a meditation excursion. I'm relieved because that last thought was not for her psychic ears.

"If we're going to do this," she says again, "we need to do this right."

For a moment, I feel like I already heard her say this, and it gives me a sense of deja-vu. I don't like it. I want to comment on this, but I feel a little dislodged. The darkest of thoughts won't leave my mind. It's growing, and I'm sinking quickly into another panic attack.

"Excuse me," I say, crashing out of the front door and making a run for it.

Thankfully, it's warm outside because I'm naked from the waist up.

I tear up my left breast on the damn bush, swing open the gate and take off.

Halfway up the street, I turn around briefly and see Astrid and Brenda standing at the gate looking after me. I wonder if there's a distance limit on Astrid's clairvoyance. I don't *want* her to hear my thoughts. I feel the terrible approach of the two bully brothers, Panic and Depression. Usually, they are accompanied by their cousins, Despair and Regret. Today is different. Today they are accompanied by the thought of doing *evil*. I can't get this horrific desire out of my head, and I'm jogging down this dark street half-naked, but it's not helping.

Run Meth. For fuck's sake, *run*, you dumb bastard.

I spontaneously start singing *Food Glorious Food* from the movie Oliver!

> *Food, glorious food*
> *Hot sausage and mustard*
> *While we're in the mood,*
> *Cold jelly and custard.*

I used to sing it during long cross-country runs as a school kid. It's something to *focus* on. *Hot sausage*, though. Fuck.

Akasuki always talked about following the breath, but sometimes that's impossible. It's claustrophobic. Sometimes. He told us not to push away negative thoughts but to allow them to come and go like clouds in the sky. Am I supposed to do this now? What about *this* dark cloud? Am I meant to allow it to come and go? What if it *doesn't* go? What if it grows into a storm? What if I —

A car beeps hard at me as I cross a small intersection without looking, and for a second, I wonder if I should just let a car hit me and put me in a wheelchair. Maybe that's the answer. Have there ever been any disabled rapists throughout history? Maybe I owe it to Brenda to paralyse myself.

Peas pudding and saveloys,
What next is the question?
Rich gentlemen have it, boys,
In-di-gestion,

I stop outside a restaurant called *Mok's Wok* and glare in at the diners scoffing down spare ribs. A couple in the window give me the look of filth, and I realise I'm a topless man with blood running down his chest. They must assume I've been in some mad fight with a Footscray junkie. I probably look utterly crazy, and I'm probably ruining their fifth wedding anniversary.

It could be worse. I could get my dick out and really ruin it for them. I want to, but why should I resent them for their happiness, even if it is only at a cheap Chinese restaurant in this shitty town?

Then *she* is there. I can't see her, but I feel her presence and her golden face looking at me from across the breakfast table. She's smiling without judgement. I never saw her angry. Not even once.

In prison, I thought about her every night and wondered if she left because I didn't deserve her. I never appreciated her.

She's telling me to breathe long and slow. I think it's *her*, but it could also be Astrid communicating telepathically. Now it sounds like Akasuki's voice or my mind is *making* it that way.

I sit on the pavement, cross my legs, and breathe slowly. I'm *just* fucking hanging on. It's a roll of the dice on where this horrific mind will go next.

I think about getting hit by the car again, only this time, in my late-night fantasy, my head shatters against a lamppost, and in an instant, I'm gone, leaving just a bag of meat for the ambulance to clean up.

Then I think of *her* head hitting the floor and her shopping pouring across the road — the oranges rolling. She loved oranges. She would squeeze them into juice every morning. Her box of muesli is torn open — malty flakes meet bitumen. A carton of soy milk dead in the gutter.

Corpus Edamame.

I return to the breath again, but my throat cramps, and I'm crying again like a child. *Fuck.* I don't know if I can do this. I must look fucking insane. Can't somebody just shoot me? Please. Breathe, for fuck's sake, *breathe, Conrad, you prick.*

"You know they *deliver* Chinese food these days, right?"

It's Astrid. She's standing at the edge of the pavement, one foot on the road.

"Yep," I say through a barrage of snot and coughing, "But you don't get that classic Chinese restaurant *ambience.*" I'm pointing into the shit restaurant at the young couple who have moved to another table.

Astrid smiles at me and throws me the cock-head shirt.

"Put that on, you twat, and let's get out of here before the cops come," she says. "You look like a fucking nutter."

As I stand up, I kneel on some chewing gum, and it stretches out like pizza dough.

"Fuck," I say, "I can see why you get your balls cut off for chewing gum in Singapore. These fucking pricks."

"I don't think they cut your balls off, you tool," Astrid says.

The legendary cock-head shirt is a purple mess. It's covered in blood and whiteboard marker, and a drizzle of dried spunk.

We walk through the steamy streets of Footscray, mostly in silence. I notice a pile of three or four used syringes and wonder if there's a bit of heroin in them.

Astrid puts her arm around me. No judgement.

"It's not worth the Hep B, *trust me*," she says.

"I don't want to be involved with the soup project," I tell her.

"I know, Nick. But Keith needs us, and I think you need to get outside of yourself. You'll come good if you do the work, and a big part of the work is getting out of your ego a bit."

My fucking ego. What the fuck is she talking about? Am I just being a selfish prick? I mean, it's easy to say when you haven't been fucked up the arse continuously or lost the only people that have ever understood you.

"Look, Nick, I get all that stuff. I get that you —"

I feel it. *I'm like Scarface in Scarface.*

"Astrid, can you please get *the fuck* out of my head? There's no fucking privacy. I need privacy, for fuck's sake. *Just leave me alone.*"

I step out and cross the road. When I turn around to apologise, she's gone. Was she even really there? She must have been since I'm wearing the purple shirt. It's hard to know what's real anymore. I'm such a cliche headcase.

I need more whiskey, but booze costs money, and people without money can't get drunk. Even Turpentine costs money — not much, but it does.

I don't even have anyone to ask for a loan, and yet these fuckers expect me to help them raise money for their soup kitchen when I don't have enough for a fucking sandwich myself. Fuck them all.

I wish I knew where that therapist lived. I bet that prick has a whole cabinet full of fine whiskey.

This is how it begins. This week, I'm learning about how rapists and thieves are born. I'm standing at the crossroads like Robert Johnson, and the devil is showing me his cock.

I don't want to go back to the gaff. Six months was enough. The thinking man's rehabilitation is working wonders for me. It's like a deranged circle. Doing time made me want to do this evil shit, yet it's the only thing *stopping* me from doing it — that, and a faint glimmer of morality leftover like that last slither of blue cheese festering in the sun after a good barbecue.

I've fucked it with Astrid, I think. She told me her secret, and I fucked her over by humiliating her. At least I know that too. I'm not totally deranged. I mean, that's what's *supposed* to happen here, right? I'm meant to fuck off everyone who tries to love me or help me before I chuck myself off a bridge or eat sixty Tramadol or something. That's the cliche. Why break with tradition? Who am I to create something new and fresh?

Besides, I'm wise to the fact that I like people because of what they give me, and I like *her* because she made me spunk on the Count's legs. There's a certain freedom in knowing that. It means I don't have to get close to anyone anymore.

I think I know what's ahead, and I don't know if there's a way around it. I want to say I wish I could heal myself, but it's not like that anymore. I don't want to heal. I want to destroy myself morally, physically, and spiritually. It's too far gone. I'm like the fucking Titanic — all those rich bastards thinking they had it made and then drowning in freezing water — it's what Akasuki would call *the inevitable suffering of the wheel of existence.*

Shit, he *did* say that.

Now I'm staring at the bottles of Johnnie Walker lined up in this booze shop called *Blackhearts and Sparrows*. My heart is black, so I take it as a sign.

There's a honk like a braying donkey as I walk in, and a Meatloaf-lookalike nods at me, despite my deranged appearance.

I peruse the shelves and select a bottle of Johnnie Walker Black — not the red stuff. I want the blue, but Meatloaf has it behind glass. I pick up a second bottle and stare into the beer fridge, pretending to look at some kind of chaser. But chasers are for twenty-year-olds with mullets and jobs — not people like me.

Meatloaf doesn't seem to give a fuck. He's looking at his phone and swiping. The bastard's probably on Tinder. I'm ninety percent sure that this isn't even his shop. He probably plays in a band or something.

I think about Astrid for a minute and wonder if she knows what I'm up to. Who the fuck am I? I'm a damn animal. I'm an ex-con. I *did* my time. Apparently, sixty per cent of inmates re-offend. And uneducated fucks think it's because they want to get back in. But that's bullshit. It's the last thing I want. I just want some damn booze.

I hoof it past Meatloaf toward the door. It buzzes like a pig with a blocked nose, and I'm out on the street. I glance back through the window, and Meatloaf is still swiping left, that beautiful bastard.

Fucking *yes*. I take off down the street with my two new friends. Fortunes can change so quickly. The local deities of Footscray are smiling down on me now. I could do with a paper bag for these bottles, though, so I don't get mugged on the way back. Maybe I should go back and ask Meatloaf for one.

I get back to the halfway house, and all the lights are off. I let myself in, silently closing my bedroom door and sitting on my mattress. I crack the first bottle of Johnnie and take a giant swig. It burns like a bastard, but I take another and another. I'm out of Longbeach, but my ashtray is filled with butts. I smoke about three and guzzle two-thirds of the bottle in under five minutes.

There's a gentle thud from the room next door and the sound of shuffling paper. Astrid is home. Why wouldn't she be?

I apologise *mentally* to her three times and ask her to join me, but there's nothing—no more thuds.

I notice a book on a small table beside my bed. It's not mine, and I never put it there. It's a tiny book with a worn red cover. I give it a sniff and guess it's from about nineteen-fifty-three. Gold letters on the spine say,

Zen Mind, Beginner's Mind

The paper inside is brown and worn. It says it's from nineteen seventy. I must be losing my touch. I turn another page, and there's an inscription:

Dear Nicholas. This is a first edition. I bought it in '71, but it's time to pass it on. I hope it brings you great wisdom. Love, Brenda.

Brenda — such a sweet woman trying to help me, and even now, after this gesture, the idea of sexually assaulting her turns me on. It's wrong. I'm a fucking *animal*.

I don't know. Maybe I should have sex with her anyway. I mean, she must be in her late fifties. She probably hasn't fucked a man for a long time.

Fuck these thoughts.

There's another gentle thud from next door, and I remember Astrid. I hope she isn't listening to my thoughts, but I'm sure she probably is.

I fucking hate myself.

I stand up, open my door quietly and sneak into the hallway.

What am I doing? Stop this fucking madness, please.

I crouch down and look under Astrid's door. It's dark.

Control yourself, for fuck's sake.

I knock gently.

"Astrid," I whisper.

There's no answer.

"Astrid, are you awake?"

There's still no sound, so I gently open the door. It's pitch black, but I go in anyway. I don't know what the fuck I'm doing. Johnnie has my cock in his vice as I wander like a blind pervert in the dark. I feel my arm hit something, and there's a *smash*.

A lamp comes on, and Astrid glares at me with wide eyes.

"What the fuck are you doing, Nick?" she says. She's gone even paler than usual, and I feel like she might be about to jump up and kick me in the teeth like Chun Lee.

It's one of those situations where it's hard to find the words. I see myself acting this way and want to rip off my nutsack as punishment.

There's a porcelain horse smashed on the floor. I know it's a horse because the head is still intact. It's a symbol, I'm sure — like in The Godfather. The rest of the body is in a hundred bits scattered across the room.

"Fuck, I'm sorry about the horse," I say.

"*Fuck* the horse. Why are you in my room Conrad?" she says.

"I just wanted to apologise about tonight. I was a real jerk. I don't need privacy. I appreciate your help, that's all."

"Look, *fuck off* back to bed, would you? I'm staying out of your head now, so you don't have to worry."

"No, I don't want you out of my head. I want you *in* my head. I think you are my only hope."

"With what?"

"With staying alive."

I think about the movie *Staying Alive* with John Travolta, and that's when I know she isn't really out of my head because she smiles.

"I'm sorry about the horse," I say.

"You already said that. It's been in my family for four generations, Nick."

"Fuck, I feel terrible," I say.

I don't feel anything at all.

Astrid breathes a long sigh, reaches out, takes my hand and pulls me into bed. She lifts the cock-head shirt over my head and off.

"You need to throw this fucking shirt out," she says. "It's cursed."

I go to say something, but she puts her finger on my lips to silence me. I'm okay with it. I'm like a newborn baby in this world, fresh and —

She shuffles down and slips the covers off her, pulling up her t-shirt and showing me her amazing body.

"Take your clothes off," she says.

I follow the order, removing my socks and jeans and then pulling my underpants off, revealing my unchartered pubic rainforest.

She flicks the light off and starts wanking me off again. Then, she pulls me on top of her and guides my invisible pecker into her soaking-wet invisible muff. I push it in, but it's too tight, and it feels like my foreskin is tearing, so I pull out and push it in again. I'm overwhelmed, and tears come, but it's dark, and she can't see me.

"It's the fucking *onions,*" I yell as the orgasm spreads through my whole body. I'm filling her up in the dark after two strokes. It *must* be a record.

I stay there for a moment, regretting my existence. Then, I pull out and lie next to her.

She's stroking my hair, and I feel like a fucking loser.

"I'm sorry," I say. "I just needed —"

She shushes me and keeps stroking my hair.

I'm asleep within seconds.

A Horse Called Remorse

We're on holiday in Bali, and I'm smoking a cigarette and working on the laptop. It's hot as fuck. *She* is swimming laps of the pool and looking beautiful. She stops before me, pushes her hair back, and flicks water at me.

"Why don't you come in, baby?" she says, "the water's gorgeous."

"*You're* gorgeous," I say, and I mean it. Her freckles always come out in the sun, but I'm only half looking. I'm more interested in the business plan before me on the laptop.

She flicks water at me again.

"Can you *not* please, Darling?" I say. Some water has gotten onto the keyboard, and I'm trying not to be a bastard about it.

She climbs out of the pool and wraps herself in a towel, walking gently around and sitting on the bench next to me.

"What are you doing?" she asks. I don't know why. She *never* asks about my work.

To my surprise, I can't tell her what I'm doing because I don't know. The screen is blank. I turn around to her, but she's different. Who — it's Astrid. She's sitting next to me, but she has an incredible tan and freckles.

"How's it hanging, McFly?" she asks.

I don't know how to answer that.

She grabs my laptop suddenly and throws it into the pool.

"What the fuck?" I say, "Are you insane?"

"*Always shoot for the moon, Conrad,*" she whispers.

And I'm back in my cell. There's torchlight outside and then the sound of the door unlocking. Then *they* are in my cell. There's the guard Runinika who likes to stand and watch next to Bob Scratchett, the bread-knife-wielding bastard.

I only got raped *once* by Taylor, technically. Since then, I consented because he's strong as fuck, and the pain is just too much when you struggle. I'm an analytics man, so I weigh up every possibility. If I resist, he goes hard, but he isn't a rape lover by trade. He just wants to spunk in my arse. If I don't fight, he's surprisingly gentle in comparison. So I lie there and try not to tense my arsehole too much as he spoons me lovingly.

He usually arrives with a small bottle of home-brand canola oil or a small tub of indefinable margarine. His dick isn't too big, and that's a relief. It still burns for the first couple of minutes, though. The whole process takes seven or eight minutes tops. He isn't one for extended lovemaking. I take his spunk in my arsehole, and it feels hot, like diarrhea in reverse. That's how I know he's a voluminous spunker like me.

I pretend he's *her*. She never had a cock, but I pretend she did and that she's making love to me. It's the only way to get through it. It's based on one of Akasuki's creative visualisation tools. Akasuki said we can transform *all* circumstances with the mind.

Taylor could at least give me a reach-around, but he won't. It's all about him. He's what you might call a selfish lover. So I wank myself off instead and start to enjoy myself strangely and shamefully.

He pulls out and leaves. The door clunks shut, and the torch lights disappear. This is my tax for being here. Sometimes I get a paper cut on the top of my arsehole. The oil, spunk, and my shit get into the cut, and it stings like a bastard.

I wake up in Astrid's bed, and I'm naked. Her clock says it's 11.15 am. I must have slept right in and missed the soup kitchen. Keith is going to be pissed off. He might charge me board after this.

There's a note on her pillow.

Hi Conrad
Hope you're doing alright today. Thanks for last night. Meet me in the wonky park at 6 pm today for meditation practice, okay? If it's raining, I'll be in the rotunda.
Love, A
X

I think about the events of last night and wonder why she's thanking me or even being nice to me. I suppose it's just the type of language used by humans who are rational and normal. I don't think she has anything to thank me for. From my memory, she wanked me off at dinner, tried to save me, disappeared when I told her to fuck off, and then accepted that I just walked into her room while she was asleep and broke her family's priceless porcelain horse. After all that, she still let me inside her, and I blew in about fifteen seconds.

It's not what I wished for. I wanted to establish myself as a tremendous lover — gentle yet firm and able to — *fuck it.* I need to go to the soup kitchen. There's an hour until lunch. I can still make it.

I feel okay. It's good to have routines. This is good. Astrid and I can become lovers and meditation partners. Maybe we can do that tantric thing where we wrap our legs around each other and meditate while we are inside each other. I want to be a hippy and burn incense. I can be a vegan, and we can grow vegetables together, and I'll grow my fucking hair and do yoga every day and get one of those slim bodies and dreadlocks and get some cosmic tattoo of an OM symbol or a picture of that elephant god.

I feel woozy as I stand up and go to put on my underpants. Then something comes over me. It's one of those divine intervention things you read about, and before you know it, I'm going through Astrid's drawers.

I open the top drawer of her dresser. It's filled with beads, crystals, a couple of bones —human or animal — and some undisclosed bottles of liquid. It's the drawer of a sorcerer rather than a hippy, and I decide to close it before I sniff some immortality serum and get jammed between realms.

The second drawer contains notebooks and a photo album. I open the album and see a young girl, which I assume is Baby Astrid. She's with an older man, possibly a grandfather, and she's carrying a young golden puppy. She looks so happy.

I turn the page and see Astrid as a teenager, absolutely off her tits at some party —probably in the nineties. I smile and turn the page to a painting of a terrible monster holding a knife and showing its fangs. I turn again quickly, and it's Astrid on some mountain, wearing a black robe and kneeling at an older woman's feet.

The third drawer I find contains her underwear. I hold up a couple of basic models like the Bonds-type stretchy knickers my wife used to wear. Then there are the lacy ones. There's a green pair — see-through, with lacy leaves on them. Within a few seconds, I'm wearing her green leafy panties. I take a look in the full-length mirror. They look fine.

I think about having a wank on her bed, wearing her panties, but it would just be too damn messy. That's the problem with being a voluminous ejaculator. Even after the activity of the last twenty-four hours, I could still pump out a metric cup of white in a single orgasm. The last thing I want is to — *fuck*. I'm so hungover I forgot about her clairvoyance again.

Fuck it. I'm leaving the panties on. I *need* this for some reason. I'm a new citizen now. Besides my leafy secret, I need to get my shit together. If I want to be with Astrid, I need to start acting *responsibly*.

◈

I get to the soup kitchen at about 12.15, and everyone is on their stations. To my horror, I'm on croutons. As I said, it's not the bread that bothers me. I'm getting over my bread fear. The horror comes from realising my crouton station partner is Lunchmore.

I walk over slowly, with my head hanging in a submissive pose. It's not because I'm afraid of him. It's my way of saying sorry for spunking on his legs.

"I'm sorry for spunking on your legs," I say as I come up.

He shakes his head and ignores me as he speeds up, breaking bread into testicle size bits. He shakes his head harder for a minute, then stops everything.

"Look, Nicholas. I consider what you did to me sexual assault. I didn't ask for your sperm on my legs last night, and I think having Astrid masturbate you at the table was entirely inappropriate. I have calmed down quite a lot, but I have to say I haven't gotten over it. How would you like it if I randomly came over your legs?"

I refrain from telling him I've had much worse things happen to me. I also refrain from telling him I'm wearing Astrid's leafy panties, although I can feel this fact taking on a consciousness of its own and desperately working to burst out of me.

"I'm sorry," I tell him. "I told the others not to stop you from attacking me with the knife. You were within your rights to attack me, and I wouldn't have fought back. I deserved to be stabbed for what I did to you."

Lunchmore shuffles awkwardly and begins breaking up the loaf again.

"Nicholas, I wouldn't go so far as to say you deserved to be stabbed for it. And I myself must apologise for attacking you last night. I have anger issues, you see. It's awful. The slightest thing triggers me, and I lose my mind and attack people. Keith and the others are like my guardians. Whenever the anger comes and I get violent, they drag me into the basement and sedate me. It's not normally every day, but it's been particularly bad lately, so it's a regular occurrence."

I relate more to Lunchmore now. Here is this man whose thoughts are totally out of control. Only he's different. His reaction is anger, while mine is fear. I have to admire him in that way. At least his reaction is assertive. Lunchmore is strong, and I'm weak. He goes on the attack while I go on the defence. He chooses to fight like a bear, and I prefer to fly like a damn spatchcock unless it's some piss-weak waiter. I could learn some things from him.

"Thanks, Count," I say. It's probably the most sincere thanks I've given anyone since I left. He's inspired me to be stronger and more assertive. It's funny that what to him is his weakness can still have a positive effect on someone else, and I wonder if my depression or panic attacks could even have the same effects as some —

What the fuck?

I drop a whole bottle of olive oil, which shatters on the floor, soaking our legs in glass and green oil. Lunchmore has his hands around my throat, digging his teeth deeply into my right arm just above the elbow. I feel his fangs sinking deeper, and I punch him in the head again and again.

"Get the *fuck* off me, you *animal,*" I scream. I knee and punch him and try to pull his arms from my throat simultaneously, but he is so damn strong. I realise why it took three people to overpower him. Blood is pouring down my arm now — and I'm slamming his head into the crouton tray. I hear his skull repeatedly bang against the metal until the croutons start turning red.

Two soup kitchen assistants try to pull us apart but fail. Finally, Brenda gets involved and puts the Count into a headlock while Scabby Andrew sticks a needle in his arm. Almost instantly, Lunchmore goes floppy, and Brenda drags him out of the room, leaving behind a trail of blood and croutons.

I look around the room in a daze. The adrenaline seems to have temporarily curbed my hangover, but I have a severe bite mark on my arm, pouring blood.

The assistants and clients who arrived early are looking at me and whispering. I'm a little surprised that some of them are giggling. It's not supposed to be a judgemental place. I think I'm in shock.

Keith comes running in.

"What the fuck happened, Pal?" he asks.

"I'm not sure. You know the Count just attacked me for no reason. He — well, maybe not for *no* reason. I mean, I spunked on his legs last night, but he seemed to be okay. We were getting along and —"

"Did he just say what I think he said?" Keith says to Andrew, and he nods.

"Did you call him *The Count* by any chance?"

"No, I don't think so. I'm pretty sure, well, maybe I did. I'm not sure."

"Well, that'll do it," Keith says.

"And listen me old China," he continues. "You might wanna change yer trousers, Son. They look a bit facked, that's all. No judgments 'n that."

I look down, and the front of my jeans are ripped open. My cock is poking out the sides of Astrid's leafy panties, along with an unreasonable amount of pubic hair. Thirty people must be witnessing this, and at least three or four have their mobile phones out filming the whole thing.

I'm the fucking circus today — hungover Nick the freak show with his green panties and hairy cock and bite mark on his arm and the croutons in his hair.

I feel pressure in my chest, and I know it will be either laughter or tears. I pray to the elephant god for laughter, but it's tears.

I'm crying like a bastard now, and Keith is holding me while Andrew is trying to pull up my jeans, but he can't. They are torn open. It's the deranged man's kilt. I'm a modern-day William Wallace — flappy fabric hanging from my waist, barely covering my rainforest cock in its green lingerie bag.

"Come on, Mate. I'll take you to the hospital," Keith says, leading me gently out the back door to his car.

Keith has a spare pair of jeans in his car, and while he drives, I try to put them on, quickly realising that only one of my legs will fit. I tell him we have to go home first, but it's too late. We're at the emergency room. I'm holding a piece of cloth to my shoulder, and I have a blanket wrapped around my waist.

I show the nurse the bite marks on my shoulder while Keith picks the last couple of croutons out of my hair. Then we sit down as instructed.

The light in here is pale as fuck. It's not quite Silent Hill, but a couple more notches, and I'd be looking out for fucking zombies at the window.

Keith is at the vending machine staring like he's choosing a wife.

A man is sitting opposite who looks like a beaver, and I wonder if he is here for mouth splinters, but he starts coughing like it's 1863, causing the young woman next to him to move down two seats with her pram.

Three seats down, there's a man with a bleeding head, making me wonder if the Count was okay. I feel sorry for the bastard now because I was hitting him pretty hard. Then again, I was trying to be nice. He was the prick that attacked *me*, and for what? Because I called him *Count*? He deserves that name, the psycho prick. I want to smash his fucking head in with a brick, the fucking —

"Got you a Mars," Keith says, handing me a cold Mars Bar and an even colder can of sugar-free lemonade.

"Sorry, it's sugar-free," he says. "I pressed the wrong button."

I shake my head, but I'm not shaking it because of the drink and the fact that he got me a damn Mars. I'm shaking my head in a general sense and hoping they give me some strong painkillers, and I can eat the fucking lot and pay some fucker to chop off my head with a blunt axe.

I shake my head again, and the young woman opposite gives me a dirty look. I want to explain that I wasn't shaking my head at her but just a general head shaking at fucking everything. Fuck this world. Fuck life.

"Fuck this shit," I say, standing up and heading for the door.

I hear Keith's protests as I leave. "Don't forget your drink 'n Mars," he says.

He follows me outside and offers me a Longbeach. Thank Christ. I didn't even realise that Longbeach is what I need. I forgot cigarettes even existed. Maybe that renders me a non-addict. I'm like a twelve-year-old smoking to be cool. Only I'm smoking to *stay* cool. If I'm smoking, I'm not thinking about killing myself or going on a damn rampage.

"So, you and Astrid then?" Keith says. He's grinning like a Cheshire Paedophile.

"Yeah, I fucking guess so." It's all I can manage. I don't want to talk about it because I feel guilty like a bastard.

"Take me home, would you, Keith?" I say.

"Look, Pal," he says. "I advise that you stay and —"

"Look, I don't give a fuck, Keith. Can you just —"

He nods and takes his keys out. The automatic doors swing open, and the Beaver man comes out. He pulls out a cigarette and lights it, then coughs up his stomach again. I've never understood how people can keep smoking through horrible coughing. Surely, there comes a point where —

"I've never understood people that smoke," I tell Keith. It's not what I meant to say, and Keith looks at me like a confused child, especially since I've been bumming Longbeach off him since I got out. I want to elaborate, but I'm numb as fuck. I might have blood poisoning or something.

◆

I'm back home now. Well, back at the halfway house. It's hardly *home*. I'm sitting on this piss-stained mattress and finishing the rest of the first bottle of Johnnie.

I'm smoking Keith's charity Longbeach and purposely leaving long butts for later. I'm a little concerned that the more I smoke Keith's Longbeach, the more I'll be in debt to him and the more I'll have to get involved in his damn project.

I've been dabbing bits of Johnnie on my bite marks, and it stings like a bastard but fuck it. It seems to work in those old cowboy movies. What's the worst that can happen? Let's say it gets infected, and I have to have my wanking arm cut off. That can only be positive, can't it? It's not quite a wheelchair, but it goes some way to keeping me out of trouble.

I'm thinking about Astrid. I've checked her room, and she's not home. I could do with some of her psychotic wisdom. I'm still wearing her leafy knickers, and I don't know why. It's some symbol like the bird on the goat's back, only this symbol has meaning. It means —

Fuck knows.

I've propped open the old lady lingerie blinds, and I'm staring at the grey sky and the rain pissing down, soaking the trees. It's badly needed. That's what the farmers would say anyway. They need it to water their crops. I need it for my sanity.

I hate the sun. The rain echoes depression and somehow makes it feel more united. The sun is like someone sticking their finger in your face commanding you to be grateful for your life when you couldn't be more resentful.

The Johnnie doesn't help, either. It helps with anxiety but not depression. Booze feeds depression like a vampire feeding blood to its pale lover. And on one level, you enjoy it, but it's dangerous because deep down, you know you *should* live. You just don't know *why*.

Akasuki would say that everything is conditioned. But if that's the case, then the thought that you should live is also conditioned. Decades of being told that death and suicide are the most shameful things take their toll. So you end up with this fake optimism that, under the Halloween costume, is shame rearing its ugly cock disguised in beautiful leafy panties.

The worst thing is I can't stop thinking. The booze keeps the anxiety at bay, but only just. The idea that I can't stop these thoughts is killing me. It's a claustrophobic hell. It makes me want to run shirtless down the street again. It makes me want to break the laws — criminal laws and moral and state laws. It makes me want to — well, you know. We already talked about that.

I'm not a rapist if that's what you are thinking. Yes, I *was* momentarily turned on by the idea of forcing Brenda to — well, at first, it felt like a force to balance out what had happened to *me*, but now Johnnie, that wise prick, is telling me that's just bullshit. It's an anarchic feeling but even more fundamental than that. I felt Brenda might reject me even though she wanted it. I felt almost like it was the *moralistic* thing to do. I mean, to force Brenda to do what she wanted but was too ashamed to do. It's the pure *insanity* of the male species.

I take another giant swig. I don't know why I'm bothering with it. I should just fucking bust into a chemist and eat a hundred valium. That ought to do the job — that should stop the fucking thoughts.

Damn, I wish Astrid was here to kick me in the cans and tell me I'm being a twat. Where the fuck is she anyway?

"*Where the fuck are you,* Astrid?"

I scream this out loud, lash out with my left foot and put it through the thin cement of the wall under the window.

Now I'm fucking crying again.

"Shut the fuck up, *you fucking fanny,*" I scream. I need to get my shit together.

I get up and almost rip the bedroom door off its hinges. Then I stomp around the house, checking all of the rooms. No one is home, so I return to Astrid's room. I lie on her bed and sniff the pillow. It smells of her, so I get my unrefined cock out again and wank passionately. But it's like giving CPR to a dead worm, so I roll over and cry into her pillow instead, and within minutes I'm asleep.

It's dark when I wake up, and I have a proper headache. I'm hungry, and I can hear voices in the kitchen. I lift myself gently off Astrid's bed, and my phone falls out of my pocket with a piece of paper.

Hi Conrad

Hope you're doing alright today. Thanks for last night. Meet me in the wonky park at 6 pm today for medit—

Fuck. What time is it? My phone tells me it's 8.21 pm. Fuck. I missed it.

Fuck.

Conrad, you *prick.* Talk about being your own worst enemy.

I have a good excuse, though. The Count attacked me, and I had to go to the hospital. Surely, she'll be concerned for me when I tell her this.

I dial her number, sitting on the edge of her bed. My eyes adjust, and I notice the head of the porcelain horse sitting atop its shattered body in a tiny white teacup.

"*Always shoot for the moon*," the horse says.

"What?" I say back. It's dark.

Hi, you've reached Astrid. Leave a message, and I'll—

Fuck. I call again.

"What do you want, Conrad?"

"I'm sorry," I say. I'm a damn cliche. I spend my life apologising, then doing the same shit.

"Yeah, you do," she says.

Fuck.

I want to tell her about the Count and the hospital and all that, but I feel like a fucking schmunk because she already knows.

"Yeah, I already know, Nick."

Fuck.

"Where are you?" I ask.

There's no answer.

"Astrid, are you there?"

"Course I'm here, you tool. What's the matter with you, Nick? Do you know?"

"I think I'm an alcoholic," I tell her. It's a lie.

"Fuck you, Nick," she says and hangs up.

I dial again. *No answer.* I dial again.

"Nick, I can't talk. I'm busy. What do you want?"

I'm crying again. Fucking fanny *bastard.*

"I just wanted to say I'm sorry." Fuck, stop apologising, you prick.

I smash the phone against her dresser. I smash it again and again. It's my head coming apart, and all the bits of the phone are the bits of my head spraying everywhere.

It's still dark, but I can see that I've smashed the horse and the teacup it was in. There are bits everywhere, and I think I'm bleeding.

I flick on the lamp. It's jarring, revealing everything — horse and phone bits everywhere, blood all over the dresser and the bed, and it's pissing from my hand.

I'm still sitting here in her leafy knickers and a giant ball of lead in my heart and throat. I'm thinking about my dog, waiting for me to come back — day after day. I can't take it. Fuck. *Help me*, please.

I slither down onto the floor like some prehistoric slimeball. I inspect the wound, and it's dripping blood but not fast enough. The end of the horse's mouth is next to my eye. I see the mouth and teeth moving again as it says,

"*Always shoot for the Moon, Nick,*" in its Southern drawl.

I would laugh. Normally I would. But I can't. I can't move. I can't do anything.

There's a knock at the door.

"Not today, thanks," I say. The door opens anyway. It's Keith, and he's holding out a phone.

"It's for you, Pal," he says. "It's Astrid". He leans down and helps me sit up on the edge of the bed.

"You're bleeding, Pal," he says.

It's true. I'm fucking bleeding.

"Hey," I say into the phone.

"Hey," she says. There's a pause. I'm about to apologise, but I take a deep breath instead. That's something. That's progress.

"Listen to me, Nick," she says, "I want you to know something."

Keith comes back into the room with piles of bandages. He kneels next to me like a greasy nurse. I switch the phone to my left hand, and he straps my right hand up.

"I bled all over your bed. And I killed your horse again. And I wore your knickers, and the Count bit me, and I stole whiskey and —"

"Nick. Shut the fuck up," she says, "I want you to listen for a bit, okay? No talking, just listening until I say so, right?"

I nod without saying anything, but she knows.

"Nick. You are a selfish twat. It's your biggest problem. In fact, I would go as far as to say it's your *only* problem. As you know, I have some insight into your mind, and I want you to recognise that since I've known you, all you have done is think about yourself."

"Surely that's not true," I say. I feel my adrenaline pumping.

"Nick, shut the fuck up," she says, "Just listen, *okay*?"

I nod again.

Keith has finished strapping me up, and now he's putting trousers on me like I'm one of those geriatric old fuckers.

"I know you are blaming everything on your wife dying, your prison assault, your dog, the Count — but I want to tell you something."

I'm ready to hear this. I straighten my back and take another deep breath to prove it.

"You were already a selfish fuck before any of that happened," she says.

It's a cup of ice-cold piss in my face.

"What you are living with, Nick, are the *consequences* of those actions. It's cause and effect. Think about it. You were so obsessed with making money, and you told yourself it was to support her. But you were already rich enough. All she wanted was for you to be present for her. But you were addicted to the game. Then you attacked a waiter because he brought you the wrong knife. The guy was getting paid a little under minimum wage, and you totally fucked up his life, and why? Because you had no awareness of him, only yourself and how much you were grieving your wife, who was on the verge of divorcing you anyway."

It's a flaming arrow piercing my entire existence.

"As a consequence, you lost your dog and ended up getting assaulted. Still, you finally get your freedom, and all you have done is fucked up the lives of others."

"I'm sorry about your horse," I say. It's a stupid thing to say.

"Fuck the horse," she says. "Keith offers you a place to live, the food off his table, a continuous flow of cigarettes and a chance to do good. Then he asks you for a small contribution to his dream, and you can't even give him an hour of your time because you are too busy thinking about sexually assaulting middle-aged women and drinking yourself into a coma."

Damn. She knows *everything*.

"Yes, but the Count," I say.

"What about him, Nick? Are you going to say he attacked you for no reason? He didn't. You called him *Count*, and you were *told not to*, but you have so little awareness that you don't even know how to listen to other people, never mind beginning to help them."

Keith is trying to pull a new white shirt on me. I put the phone down to my waist for a minute and let him put it on. He looks like a deranged skinny speed-head monkey. But she's right. His heart is open. He is what Akasuki would call a sage. But I was too busy trying to find his faults to notice what he was doing for me.

Tears flow down my face as he buttons up my snow shirt. I look him in the eyes and desperately want to thank him, but the words are not forming. The shame is blocking the thanks.

He looks and smiles, unlike a speed addict, and he nods as if he knows. Then he puts a hand on my cheek, stands up and leaves.

I lift the phone to my ear again.

"*Fuck* the horse," I say. "I'm sorry I didn't turn up to our meditation."

Something feels honest about that.

"Listen, Nick," Astrid says. "I'm staying up north for a couple of weeks so I won't be around."

I know that hurts at some level, but I can't feel anything.

"Why don't you stay in my room?" she says, "Look after things for me? I'll be back in town for the retreat."

"The retreat?" I say, trying to act normal. "Is that happening?"

"Well, yes. You would know that if you were involved."

"Okay," I say. This conversation feels like a divorce. It feels like she's departing.

"For fuck's sake, Nick. There you go again — just thinking about your pain. *Listen* to what I'm saying. Don't focus on how hurt you are. Focus on the method I'm pointing out to you."

"There's a method?"

"Yes, Nick. *Selflessness*," she says, and she hangs up the phone.

I just sit there for a minute, numb but taking it all in.

There's another knock at the door, and Brenda pops her head in.

"Hello, Nick. Don't you look nice?" she says.

I burst into tears again, and she sits beside me, putting her arms around me and hugging me like my mother.

I'm about to apologise, but I don't. I've done enough apologising for one day.

"Thanks, Brenda," I say.

She nods.

"Okay, now come and get some stew," she says.

The Way of Zen

Today feels special.

I'm lying in Astrid's bed, looking at the ceiling. It's 1:45 pm, and last night during stew, Brenda invited me to her Zen group, which starts at 2:30 pm.

Usually, I'd start the day with a good wank, but not today. The idea that Astrid knows my every move puts me off. I'm also hungover as fuck, and I have a pain in my balls. So I put on my best cocaine shirt instead, along with the chinos Keith dressed me in last night. He left me a pair of flappy sandals as well which I slip on even though Brenda said there's no need for shoes where we're going.

I hope it's not too damn religious or anything. I've seen Zen monks making tea at an excruciatingly slow pace in their black robes. I don't think I could handle that kind of thing. I'd end up grabbing the teapot or screaming, *'Pour the fucking tea already.'*

Brenda is in the kitchen sipping on chai. I know it's chai because there's the distinct smell of camel spunk in the air.

She offers me some.

"Nah, I'm fine, Brenda," I say.

"Are you sure, Nick?" she says. "It might keep you alert during the session."

Fuck it. I suppose it's better than whiskey, which would have been my first drink of choice this morning had it not mysteriously disappeared from my room. Somewhere a fairy is legless on the proceeds of my criminal life. Damn it, Meatloaf. I'm sorry I let you down.

My second choice is coffee.

"Is there any coffee?" I ask, and Brenda's face turns to a look of disappointment. Why would she give a fuck? Is coffee against her religion? Do Zen people not drink coffee? For fuck's sake I —

I hear Astrid's voice echoing in my head. It's just one damn word — *selflessness.*

It could be the memory of our conversation last night. Or, it could be Astrid sending me psychic messages. It's hard to tell anymore.

Fuck it.

"Yeah, alright, I'll try the chai," I say to Brenda, whose face lights up as she pours a cup of the stinking brew into a mug that says *World's Best Dad.*

Is she taking the piss? Does she know me and my wife were trying to conceive? Is she trying to push my buttons like that fucking waiter? She's staring at me now. Is she waiting for me to drink and comment on the delicate balance of the spices and the honey, or is she waiting to see if I throw it in her face and beat the shit out of her with the cup?

I see her face turn to a look of concern.

"Are you okay, Nick?" she says.

I have to remember how sweet she is. I take three deep breaths and have a swig. Yep, it still tastes like camel spunk.

I nod at Brenda and say,

"It's delicious."

It's probably the first time I've ever used the word *delicious*. But I'm starting fresh in this world, like a newborn baby, selfless and — I don't know. Are newborn babies selfless? I doubt it. They have someone else do *everything* for them. Even if they wanted to be selfless, they couldn't be. They have zero chance of self-sufficiency. It's compulsory communism. Is communism the basis of all life? It has to be.

"These thoughts never shut the fuck up, do they?" I say to Brenda, and she kills herself with laughter. I don't know what's so damn funny. She probably wouldn't be laughing if she knew I almost threw boiling tea in her face and beat her to death with a World's Best Dad mug. Now *that* would be something. Life is interesting sometimes. At least it's not dull. At least it's not —

"Take that with you, Nick," Brenda says, "Are you ready?"

I'm *not* ready.

◆

Brenda's car is stupid. It's this tiny red thing like Postman Pat's van. I'm thinking about sex with Brenda again, and I don't know why. She isn't even attractive, and she must be almost sixty, but if she pulled over now and just took off her knickers, I'd definitely be up for it.

My hangover isn't helping. I always get horny when I'm hungover. But there's a picture of an Asian man hanging from her rearview mirror, and he is looking at me as if to say, *keep your hands to yourself, you piece of prison meat.*

Or, maybe that's my conscience.

I wish he hadn't said prison meat. It makes me think of Arsehole Taylor sliding his meat into my swollen, stinging backside, and now I'm breathing deeply and thinking about changing the subject.

Not that it was even a conversation.

"I think you will like this class," Brenda says. How the fuck would she know? It's not like she even knows me at all. I mean, she's seen me cry, and that's quite intimate, but my personality — she knows fuck all about my personality.

"Oh yeah?" I say. I'm trying to be selfless, but so far, I hate myself for it. I'm mentally smashing my head open like the damn porcelain horse. For a moment, I feel like punching Brenda in the face and making her crash the car, but I keep breathing. I don't think I can do selflessness. It's making me feel violent.

Brenda senses something is up, and we don't speak for a few minutes. Then, as we pass a stinking old pub, she opens up.

"My husband and I used to go to that pub," she says.

"Oh yeah?" I say again. I realise I just said it before. I want to elaborate but can't think of anything else.

"Yep," she says, "He died two years ago."

Fuck. Brenda. What am I meant to say next? Do I ask how it happened? Do I offer my condolences? I used to know these things. I would have had a statement for such a situation back in the day that I learned from some podcast.

"Do you want to have sex, Brenda?" I say. It's the absolute last thing I wanted to come out of this cursed mouth hole. I was trying to ask how it happened, but my brain got scrambled, and now my face is going redder than this Postman twat shitmobile.

"I'm sorry," I say. "I never meant to say that."

She still hasn't said anything. Either she's thinking about it, or she's too shocked to say anyth—

"Nick," she says. "I'm very flattered and grateful for your offer."

I'm getting rejected by a middle-aged woman.

"I'm sorry," I interrupt again, "I meant to ask about your husband, but that just came out. It's so rude."

I mean that. I'm not just saying it. I don't want to hurt Brenda. Is this it, Astrid? Is this what selflessness is? Is this what I need to nurture? Is this the method?

"In my experience Nick," Brenda says, "things don't usually come out unless a person is thinking about them."

Damn it, she's got me there. Maybe she *isn't* going to reject me.

"I used to be so beautiful back in the day," she says.

I see that. There *is* something beautiful about her, especially when she smiles.

"I used to be a dancer in my early twenties," she says, "not an exotic dancer, but professional still. I had an amazing body, and men used to always look at me. That's when I met my husband. He was a police officer. I met him on the eve of his wedding to his first wife."

"What's that?" I say. She has a cheeky smile, and I can see the attractive young dancer in her face. I notice I'm smiling as well. Now *there's* a rare creature — the Nick Conrad smile. Someone call fucking Attenborough.

"So he broke off the wedding to be with you?" I say.

It's like some reality TV show. I don't know why I'm so damn interested, but I am, and it feels like serotonin is coming out of my brain and pouring into my cheeks. Is this what selflessness is? Is this what I need to nurture? Is this the method? As soon as I analyse it, it turns to depression. Why? I know. It's because I made it about *me* again.

Fuck. It *must* be the method.

"No, they didn't break it off," Brenda says. "They were married for two years. Joe and I didn't see each other again until eighteen months later. That's when we started the affair. He was so well hung, Nick. It was such a shock for me being so young. I'd hardly slept with any men. It was painful initially, but I soon realised I couldn't let this man go."

Now I'm fucking laughing, and it's authentic. What is this phenomenon?

"So you fell in love with his cock?" I say.

She is laughing even harder than me.

Then there's silence for a minute, and Brenda says,

"The love part of it came later, Nick. I've never loved someone so much in my whole life. The pain of losing someone like that is so shocking and leaves you — well, you know. I'm sorry if this is triggering things for you."

It's not triggering anything, and that's also a first. My hard-on is gone, and I'm only concerned about Brenda's well-being. I'm not even thinking about my situation. This must be the method. I hope it's not. I don't want there to be a method. This is just too damn *pure*.

I take a deep breath.

"How did it happen, if you don't mind me asking?" I say. It's probably the most normal thing I've said in a year.

"Cancer," she says like she has answered that question a hundred times. "Cancer of the gall bladder, not one of those *commercial* cancers."

She smiles at her cancer joke, and I smile back without my teeth.

"I'm sorry, Brenda," I say. This time I mean it. I'm not just sorry for her husband's cancer. I'm sorry for wanting to sexually assault her. I'm sorry for fantasising about beating her up with a World's Best Dad mug.

"Thanks, Nick," she says.

We pull into a gravel driveway and through a large wooden gate, parking in a beige car park under the shade of a single tree. It's bloody hot as we exit the Postman Pat van and crunch-walk up to what looks like a rich person's house.

It's cool inside as Brenda slips off her shoes, and I drop off Keith's flappy sandals. We walk on shiny white tiles and into a large, tranquil room with a giant white Buddha statue surrounded by flowers up the front.

A few people are already seated in there. Some sit cross-legged on the ground, some kneel on these little wooden stools, and some sit in chairs.

"I think I'm gonna go for a chair," I say loudly.

Brenda is already making her way up the front toward the extreme cross-legged people.

A few people turn and look at me with scowls. One younger man in Harry Potter glasses and a kaftan hushes me with his index finger.

I want to jump on the fucker, take off his glasses and ram them down the prick's throat.

"*Go fuck yourself,*" I say to the man. He turns a pale white colour and looks toward the front. "Meditate on that, you Griffindor *twat,*" I say, walking toward the chairs at the back.

Once the room fills up, I quickly notice the hierarchy here. The men with shaven heads and black robes are up the front, though strangely, they are *not* Asian men. They probably have Asian names like Akasuki still, but in reality, it's good Christian names — Chris, John. There might even be a Sven or Anders or maybe a Dutch name like Hendrik or Pieter or —Anyway, there are no women in the front row. They are all sitting behind. We chair sitters are all at the back, like losers. You don't deserve to be upfront if your legs aren't flexible. The hierarchy must be about the legs and whether you have a cock.

A bell rings, and everyone stands up. Then, a door opens, and an old Asian man shuffles into the room, being held up by another Asian man in a black robe. I wonder if it's the Asian monk hanging in the rear mirror of Brenda's car — the bastard that called me *prison meat*. But you can't tell. Old Asian monks all look the same to me. And sure, you *can't* make comments like that anymore without some prick pissing their damn pants and calling you a racist. But I'm sure it goes both ways. Isn't it harder for people to distinguish differences in people that aren't their own race? It's not like there's any *hatred* in that, but some people just wet their knickers at the first opportunity to point out prejudice. They'll search hard to find a reason why it's wrong, not because it is but because they desperately *want* it to be.

Anyway, fuck it. None of that matters. Again, you probably think I'm that romper stomper nazi Russell Crowe prick again, but I'm not. It's about *authenticity* to me. How many of those white monks kept their Western names? Why the fuck are they shaving their heads and wearing robes. Why the fuck are they all upfront. I mean, why can't they fucking mingle in the next section? If I were a monk, I would sit in a chair just to piss everyone off.

From what I've seen so far, this is a *very* religious ceremony — nothing like the non-religious plainness Brenda sold it as last night during stew. I feel like the victim of fraud.

My stomach rumbles when I think about stew. I should have eaten something beforehand. It's not easy to sit and do fuck all on an empty stomach.

And all this time, the monks are *still* walking toward the front at that teapot pace, and I'm getting antsy. And now Brenda is waving me over like she wants me to come and sit up the front. And after all my ranting about wanting to break the hierarchy and all that, I'm just smiling and mouthing *no* at her.

But now her friend turns around and waves me over too. Obviously, Brenda needed permission from the hierarchy to get me in there, which took some time. I mean, I have the cock but not the right legs, so I guess I should be honoured.

Astrid is whispering about the method in my ear, and I don't give a fuck whether it's her or not anymore. I stand up, awkwardly moping forward, over a line or two of humans sitting perfectly cross-legged. There are a few mutters and tuts, and I realise too late that I'm probably meant to enter each row from the side. Fuck it. For a bunch of Zen students, these pricks don't seem very Zen, whatever that means.

Brenda and her friend move apart to make a space between them about half the width of my body. What I thought was a cushion is more like a flat square piece of sponge. I lower myself onto it. Now I have to cross my legs. I should have thought this through better.

My legs are crossed, alright, but I wouldn't describe myself as comfortable. My knees are fucking hurting already, and I feel physically unbalanced. I'm holding myself up with my lower spine. Both my knees and back are killing me, and I've been in this position for about fifteen seconds.

Why can't they just give you proper cushions or a damn fucking baked bean bag?

Now I'm sitting like a bellend between these two middle-aged women, and I'm sweating from discomfort, and the bastard teacher and his assistant *still* haven't made it to the front. I'm not sure if I can fucking do this. Akasuki talked about Zen being a vigorous practice but not like this. It's downright torture, for fuck's sake.

Brenda's friend is a little younger than her. She has a whiff of attractiveness, and she has oversized breasts. I've always been a *sucker* for an oversized breast. It's a primordial thing. So I keep nudging my eyeballs sideways to glance at the surprisingly perky love mountains. She has a scent too. It smells like sage mixed with smoked vagina. I like it, and I get the urge to sit in her lap and suck on her ample bosom like it's day one, and I'm back at the start, able to begin again and revise my life, skipping all the regretful parts and avoiding the —

DING

That's another bell, in case you are wondering, and I almost jump out of my fucking ghostly shell and into the next realm.

The old monk is on his throne now, and his assistant is sitting on the floor next to him, and everyone stands up and starts bowing down, touching their heads to the ground while he sorts through his damn papers or whatever.

I never expected *this*.

Brenda said this wasn't religious, and yet, at this current time, it's more religious than your average church.

I don't want to bow down. I'm sure there is a good reason for it but isn't the point supposed to be something about equanimity? How can there be true peace while there is still a hierarchy? I didn't read that from some book either. It just seems logical.

Anyway fuck it, my back and knees are about to burst into flames, so I take it as an opportunity to stand up and stretch my legs. Then, I bow down like the others and slowly headbutt the ground. It's harder than it looks. I do my fourth one and stand up. It feels good— like it's flexing my knees and my back. I go for a fifth, but Brenda grabs my shirt.

Damn it, Brenda, I was just —

She tells me we are only meant to do it three times, and I ask why. She says something about jewels, which I don't quite understand.

I ask her if it has anything to do with De La Soul, but I only get to *La* when the old monk coughs loudly into a microphone. It's a real phlegmy cough — quite foul.

It's funny how religious people get away with such foul throat clearings. He could have turned away from the microphone to do it. It's almost like he wanted to disgust everyone by amplifying his phlegmish activity and swallowing the lot.

He muffles on about something in an Asian language for an unacceptable time. I want to put my hand up and tell him that no one can fucking understand what he is saying and that he probably needs a translator or something.

I'm looking around while I think this, but no one else seems to give a fuck. Brenda and Perky Love Mountains both have their eyes closed, and Perky is even nodding like she knows what the fuck he is saying. I don't know. Maybe she speaks the language.

Fuck my fucking knees. I'm not sure if I can —

There's a ruffling of another microphone, and the monk assistant does the same phlegmish cough and then says,

"The Master welcomes you all once again. The Master is happy that you could all make it and that it is due to our karma and past aspirations that we are able to join together and practice here again and again."

I'm looking at the Master, and I have to say that he doesn't look happy to be here at all. He looks like someone just stole his prize Bonsai tree.

"So, we will begin by chanting the threefold refuge prayer three times," says the assistant monk, "Then we will sit Zazen for around half an hour."

I know what Zazen is. Akasuki used to talk about it. It seems to mean *doing fuck all* or something like that.

I have no idea what this refuge prayer is, and I'm a little pissed off that they don't give you a bit of paper with such things on like they used to do at church when I was little.

"When you sit —" says the monk. "sit like a mountain. Be unshakable. Express your Buddha nature. Sit like a Buddha."

I'm fairly certain Buddha does *not* sit like I am right now. I'm hugging my knees, and my whole fucking body is burning.

I start to realise there's a hierarchy for a reason. Every one of these people is sitting there quietly. Their knees are all touching the ground while mine are all strung up in the air like the sails of a damn ship. And now my stomach is blowing up like a fucking balloon.

Holding my knees into my chest makes me want to off-gas, but the heat in my gut tells me it's the worst idea in the world. It's the chai. I don't know what they put in that stuff — probably too many damn beans — but it's *not* good for meditation.

"In zazen, it is important that your body is comfortable," says the monk. "That is why we need a stable posture that is unshake-able. When the body is comfortable, it is free to fall away."

There's no fucking chance my body is falling away unless I die from the pain in my knees and back and now my stomach. I wonder if you can die from holding in gas. I might need to release it. *No.*

I lean across to Brenda and whisper in her ear. She jumps a fucking mile because she had her eyes closed, listening to the dulcet tones of the assistant monk.

"I might just sit back in my chair," I say. I want to explain that my knees and back are in pain, and my stomach is like a fucking beach ball and that I think that if I stay, I might not be able to stop looking to my right at Perky's love mountains, but she wouldn't understand. So, I finish on the word *chair*.

She says nothing but nods once and closes her eyes again. It's what I needed. No judgement. I turn round to nod at Perky one more time. That's what I tell myself anyway. In truth, I'm just having one more look at her breasts.

I lean back, put my hand on the ground and push myself onto my knees. As I do, I feel the gas release. It's a C note on an oboe, but I continue my ascent. As I do, a second, more earthy tone comes out. This time it's a D flat. It's a minor second interval like the intro to Jaws. It's appropriate because the stinking shark is about to creep up on these people in a way that might traumatise them forever.

The standard operating procedure here is to stay very still, like when you see a snake. But our human instinct says, *Run, Motherfucker, Run.*

It's too late. I'm on my feet, and my sharky honk has alerted people to my movement.

I know from the exit heat that it will be a horrific chai fart, but I keep moving, like a warrior set on his goal, regardless of the consequences.

Once again, I remember too late that I'm supposed to go around the side of the rows, and I hover my arse over all the citizens instead, like I'm unleashing an airborne chemical weapon.

I outrun the stink, but gas follows its maker as if it is attached by some mysterious stink cord. We all know that you have to cut it off, and I have failed. Now, as the decrepit poison fills my nostrils, I do not doubt that it has served the entire room.

Everyone's eyes are still closed, and I must do the same now. At least I'm in a chair. It feels so damn good to be off the floor.

The bell rings again, and I realise the monk has stopped talking. What was it he said again? Ah, yes. Zazen. Do fuck all for half an hour. Fine by me.

I sit there for a few moments thinking about Akasuki. He used to tell us to follow our breath but not in a tense way.

He said, *casually watch the breath like* — what was it again? *Like a farmer watching a sheep* or something — or *like an otter watching a fish* — *a fish watching a prawn*, or *a prawn watching a* — I can't remember—some shit.

I focus on my breath for now, but whenever I relax, the girl three seats down from me coughs. I sneak a look to see if she's attractive. I could forgive her coughing if she's pretty, but I can't see her because the man between us is so fat.

Damn, there she goes again. That's cough number five, I believe. What's the point in coming to a silent meditation session if you are going to cough all the way through like a fucking Bronchiosaurus Rex or whatever?

I wake up to the bell and realise I've drooled down my cocaine shirt.

"Was I snoring?" I ask the fat man. He smiles and tells me I only snored for the last five minutes.

I head outside, and Coughing Girl is sitting on a wall smoking. My intention is good as I head over, but I have no control over the words as they exit.

"Thanks for keeping everyone awake with your coughing," I say.

"No problems. Thanks for keeping everyone awake with your farting," she says.

That brilliant fucking bitch. I never saw *that* coming.

"Besides," she continues between coughs, "you're not supposed to be sleeping in there. It's not a sleeping class. Technically keeping you awake from a meditation standpoint would be a good thing."

I have no idea what she's talking about. Is she talking about enlightenment? Don't you have to be an Asian male with a good cock and legs to experience that?

I stand there staring like a weird fucker, trying to think of some brilliant comeback.

What the fuck would she know anyway? I mean, she's sitting there smoking and coughing. How enlightened could she possibly be?

She stomps on her cigarette with her tatty shoes and fucks off before I can say anything else out loud. And I'm just left standing there with my mouth hanging open like the channel tunnel. I was about to ask her out, I think.

I wasn't. Once again, I forgot I'm not American.

Fuck it. I wouldn't mind a drink and a Longbeach.

I should wait for Brenda and get introduced to Perky so I can stop calling her Perky. It's derogatory. I know that.

If Astrid were here, she would punch me in the cock. Damn, I wish she was here to punch me in the cock. Fuck. Anyway, I can't hang around. I'm feeling depressed again like the Zen session has triggered me. My stink bomb was just too much. There's no way I can stick around to greet my public after that performance.

I don't know where I am, and I don't even have a phone to find out since I smashed the shit out of it last night.

So I walk instead.

I know I can't keep living like this. I want to get my shit together. Just keep fucking breathing, you idiot. Fuck, I feel it coming — the school bully — the hot and cold sensation. I think it's fine, isn't it? Everything is fine.

Fuck, I need some booze, but I have no money, no car, and I don't know where the fuck I am. I should go back to Brenda. But then I'll have to face the crowd, or at least Perky — or whatever her name is. I don't know — Brenda's friend.

It's *selflessness*. It's the method. I should do it. I should go back to overcome my ego. It's the thing to do.

Brenda is standing next to a long table with tea, an assortment of biscuits, and small sandwiches.

"Hi, Nick," she says. "We thought you'd disappeared on us."

"I wish," I say, noticing the sandwiches in particular.

"I had no idea there would be sandwiches," I say, desperately trying to hold it together. I try to smile, but it feels more like a grimace.

Perky makes a terrified face for a microsecond before correcting it and smiling at me.

"Nick, this is Berthandra," Brenda says.

"I'm sorry?" I say. I swear she just said *Berthandra*.

"I'm Berthandra," says Perky, holding out her hand.

I shake her hot hand while holding my attention on her face, away from her chest, which takes extreme meditative concentration.

"That's an interesting name," I say. What I mean is it's a stupid fucking name. Who names their child Berthandra, for fuck's sake? I realise there's always a chance now that anyone I meet could be psychic like Astrid. I guess I'll know if Berthandra slaps my face. I squint and wait for impact.

Astrid's voice is in my head again.

It's not very selfless to slag off someone's name like that, Nick.

She's right. I mean, who can help their name? It's not like it's her fault. She must have fucking dumb parents.

"Yes, I had a re-naming ceremony when I was twenty-six," says Berthandra. "Berthandra came to me during a ceremony in Peru."

"That's great," I say with another grimace.

"Would you like a biscuit?" says Brenda.

I know she senses trouble because I'm emitting the stench of trouble like my arsehole emitted the horrific stench back in the Zen hall. And I realise now that no one has mentioned that or remembered it, and I even forgot it myself for a while.

It's a Christmas miracle. Do they even have Christmas in Zen? Of course, they don't. What a stupid idea. It's more likely people are being non-judgemental or selfless. They are practising the *method.*

I turn down the biscuit and the subsequent sandwich. It's not because I have bread fear either, if that's what you're thinking. It's because I've turned my attention to a crowd of four or five people whispering non-non-judgementally over there.

At the heart of the crowd is the man with Harry Potter glasses, who I told to go fuck himself. He is flanked by a tall woman who looks like she's going to come over and give me a stiff one, so I get ahead of the crowd and give her a deep scowl and my middle finger. It's what you call a pre-emptive strike. You have to get in first to protect your —

"Nicholas!" Brenda says.

I'm back home with my mum, getting fucking told off for wearing her underwear. And yeah, I know you're joining the dots and piping up like some lingerie Miss Marple. You're a motherfucking genius, okay.

Brenda has pulled me to one side and is giving me the stink eye.

"Nicholas, this is my group. These people are my friends, and I trusted you enough to bring you along. You can't go giving people the finger."

"She started it," I say. "She was glaring at me like she was about to take me down with her massive arms."

"Nicholas, calm down for a minute," Brenda says. "For starters, Anthony is not a *she*. Anthony is a *he* — a man."

"Oh, for fuck's sake," I say.

This is one of those times where I have to play along with the fucking game because it's the method.

"Fine," I say. "*He* was staring at me like *he* wanted to put me in a fucking ju-jitsu hold."

"I don't think so," Brenda says. "Anthony is the nicest person. Why would you think that?"

"It's because I told Harry Potter to go fuck himself," I say.

Brenda looks confused now, but she needn't be for much longer because Harry and lanky Anthony Weasley come over and join us.

"Oh, fucking *great*," I roar.

"Nicholas, this is Anthony and Jeff," Brenda says, "Guys, this is —"

"Draco Malfoy," I say, interrupting her. "And what do you want, *Potter*?"

"Nicholas!" Brenda exclaims again.

I get why she's shocked. Even I'm shocked at my behaviour if I'm honest. But isn't Zen supposed to be a spontaneous art? That's what Akasuki used to say, and that bloke Allan Watts when I read one of his books in the gaff.

"Just the two of you, is it?" I continue. "Where is Miss Granger?"

I know they came over to report my *go fuck yourself* comment to Brenda, but now it just seems ridiculous. Had I been nice in our latest encounter, the previous comment would have been shocking, but given this latest outburst, it seems totally in line with my current behaviour.

"You're a rude little man!" Anthony Weasley blurts out, towering over me like the grim reaper.

"Yeah? Well, at least I'm a *real* man," I say.

It's a cheap shot, I know. I don't even care about gender at all. I just know, at some level, he is bound to have *some* trauma about his gender, and I want to pull it out to hurt him.

I see a flash of sadness in Anthony's eyes, and I feel so damn sad for him, and I fucking hate myself. I mean, twenty-four hours ago, I stole my girlfriend's green panties. What's that? Did I say, girlfriend? Fuck, I don't know why I w—

"*OOOF,*"

It's the same oof I used to make when Arsehole Taylor entered me. Now it's because Weasley laid one on my jaw. I assume so anyway because for a second, I blacked out, and now he has me in some ju-jitsu hold. That was a hell of a prediction. Maybe I'm developing psychic powers like Astrid. It must be all the meditation I'm doing.

"Now, who's a real man, fuckhead?" Anthony says.

"Get off me, you *twat*," I say.

I seriously can't fucking breathe here. Come to think of it, this is good. Just keep strangling, you lanky prick. I'll die, and you'll go to prison and get fucking reamed like I did. It's a win-win.

Two of the others pull Anthony off, and now I'm just sitting there. Brenda is crouched next to me, asking if I'm alright.

In the words of Marcellus Wallace,

Nah, Man. I'm pretty fucking far from okay.

But I don't tell Brenda that.

There's a fucking rage boiling up from within me. I'm scanning the room for sharp objects. There's a pile of spoons on the table, and yeah, you might think a spoon isn't sharp, and you would be right about the round part, but the handle — those handles can pierce the softest part of a human body — the eyeball, the neck, the armpit, parts of the foot can be devastated by a spoon handle.

My body is filling with fire. I'm staring one-pointedly at Anthony's neck. I'm calculating how quickly I can get to a spoon and ram it in the prick's neck before anyone knows what's happening.

I'm fairly quick. I had to learn to be fast in the gaff. I clench my fists and hands like steel fucking springs about to launch myself.

Brenda puts her arms around me. She pulls herself in tight, and I'm in a trance. Berthandra crouches and holds me from the other side, pushing her massive breasts into me.

I feel warm and something like being loved. I'm back in the hot, red womb. You don't realise how cold you have felt your whole life until you have one of those moments. You become so used to being rejected after your fuck ups that you become so afraid of fucking up, which kills your range of motion.

I want to enjoy it, but it's covered in the spunk of shame. I hate myself for feeling loved. The rage is melting like a fucking cream cake in a fire, and I'm fucking crying again like a —like a — like a — *Fuck*.

I want to get drunk. I want to get shitfaced and have a threesome with Brenda and Berthandra. I want to fuck their tits and their pussies and their arses and fucking spunk down their god damn throats and *FUCK*. I know this feeling. It's back. Fuck. This is how it happens. I can't stop it. It's out of control. My thoughts are out of control.

I push both the women off me, stand up and kick the table hard, sending biscuits and cucumber sandwiches flying. Then I turn around and sprint out of the door.

I'm running down the street now, but I have no fucking clue where I am. I'm running away from *Rapist Gump*, but he's following me, the mad pervert. How do you run away from your mind? It's fucking horrible. Fuck. Everything was going so well. I should remember the method — *selflessness* —no, fuck selflessness. I've been practising it all day, and look where it got me. Selflessness is the source of all these problems.

I stop in the street and stand there. I should go back and fuck that lanky rat up with a spoon. I should stab his skinny fucking neck again and again.

I imagine it in my head — the black blood pissing everywhere — a look of sheer terror in the eyes. That's right, you pissant — *I'm* the sourdough king. I'm the one that was in the fucking gaff. I'm the one that fucks *you* up, not the other way around. Now, who's the real man, eh? *Eh? EH?*

Brenda pulls up next to me in the Postman Pat wagon.

"Get in, Nick," she says.

I start walking again, saying nothing.

"Nicholas, get in the CAR!" she demands.

Fuck it.

So, I get in, and now we're riding home, and we're saying nothing.

"I'm sorry, Bren," I say, shortening her name in desperation.

I'm not sorry.

"Look, I know my behaviour is shocking," I say.

She laughs her out-of-control laughter.

"Shocking?" she says, mocking me. "I've worked in the soup kitchen for four years, Nick. I've broken up more fights than you could imagine. I've been called every name under the sun. I've been molested by clients. I've been —" She pauses for a few seconds. "It's

not shocking, Nick. I've seen it many times. I want to help you.
I just don't think you know how to help yourself."

It's a damn cliche, but she's fucking right. I don't even know
if it's *possible* to help me anymore. I can feel my descent into
madness —into becoming a violent criminal, and I don't know
how to stop it.

◆

We pull up outside the halfway house.

"I have to go to the shops," Brenda says. "We can talk later."

I know that means to get the fuck out, so I do.

The sun's baking again, urging me to enjoy life and be a better
person. I'd forgotten about my anxiety, but now it's coming back
with a side of guilt. This whole day's been a blur.

"Nick," Brenda says, winding down the passenger window. I
turn around. There she is, the celestial dinner lady. What words
of fucking wisdom will she pour at me now from one of her books
or Asian monk teachers?

"It's going to be okay, Nick," she says, smiling.

"*I doubt it*," I say.

I pull my room apart, looking for the second bottle of Johnnie.
I'm pissed off that some fucker took it. Maybe it was Keith, that
skinny prick or Brenda or —

I stomp outside to the recycling and see two Johnnie Black
bottles lying empty on the top. Why do people have to fucking
interfere with their fucking methods? I've got *no chance* now.
I'm destined for oblivion.

Back inside, I spot Keith's Thermomix just sitting there, begging to be stolen. I'm generally not a thief, but sometimes there's a necessity for such things. I reason that selling Keith's Thermomix will help sedate me and stop me from stabbing people with spoons.

I notice too that Keith's car keys are hanging there invitingly. He must be at the soup kitchen since it's the only place he walks to. I think again about what Astrid said about Keith and the things he did for me. The neo-rational side of my brain says that if Keith were here, he would be fine about lending me his shit-cream Falcon and Thermomix despite them being his two most precious possessions.

Why don't you call him then? comes Astrid's voice. I spin around, but she isn't there.

I'm fucking losing it here. It can't be her — not right now — it's just far too inconvenient.

This is one of those freight train situations where you know something is happening, and nothing can get in the way. There's no point in analysing it any further. Besides, how can there be right and wrong if everything is conditioned? It's *selflessness*.

Sure, I might be acting selfish, but if selflessness is the method, isn't it being selfless to allow Keith to be selfless toward me? How can anyone else practice the way if there is no selfishness? It's a fair question.

I grab Keith's car keys and take his Thermomix to the shit-cream Falcon. It doesn't smell like dick cheese anymore. It smells like vanilla. For a moment, I wonder if it ever smelled like dick cheese or if that was something to do with my perception. That day, in Footscray, getting picked up by the skinny bastard seems so long ago. But it was barely three weeks ago.

I drive about six kilometres to a series of shops where I know there's a pawn shop. On the way, I remember the therapist and how he gave me alcohol and cigarettes and let me sleep. That's proper therapy —letting people be, not fucking hassling them and thinking your solution is their solution.

If some bastard hadn't taken my Johnnie, we wouldn't be in this situation. And yeah, part of me knows that's a delusion. I've heard it from myself too many times, but it's convenient for what is happening now.

It's all my fucking fault. I know that.

I think that's why today feels special. It feels like the day. And yeah, our Lamborghini monk mentality might take that to mean that it's a day of healing. But that's not what I mean. It's too late for that.

Wanting to heal, wanting to feel better, that's fucking selfish crap. Being selfless means thinking of others, and honestly, I believe now that I'm a danger to others and therefore need to be removed.

Putting others' safety before my own is the method.

That's why today is special.

I'm going to fucking kill myself.

That's *true* selflessness.

That's the way of Zen.

The Carcinogenic Countdown

This pawn shop stinks. They've washed the carpet, so there's this fucking odour of harsh toxic chemicals. I want to ask the owner if he has any lying around that I can drink, but I get distracted by the DVDs. Who the fuck even still has a DVD player these days? These discs won't be flying off the shelves.

I see 'The Towering Inferno' and 'The Fly' next to each other. I take it as a sign because they were the first VHS I shoplifted in my teens. The third was RoboCop.

They were days of luminous hope when my friends and I would steal video cassettes, sell them in a shop called Riverside Records and spend the proceeds on cannabis and arcade games. I'd say it was a simpler time, but that's just another damn fucking cliche, and I know you can't stand them because you don't get that life is one massive fucking cliche yet.

The carpet isn't really why this shop reeks. It stinks of the flaws of capitalism. It reeks of the lower end of the see-saw. It reeks of a society committed to rewarding those that *can* and punishing those that *can't*. Somebody once loved those DVDs. Every TV here smells of a father with a gambling addiction or a heroin addict in need.

The owner of the shop looks like Jeffrey Lebowski. He is the fucking Dude if the Dude had been eating 24/7 for the last decade. I don't know how people can get that fat. Surely there's a point where you think *I can't fucking keep eating*, right?

Wrong. This man is no different to gambling addicts, drug addicts, alcoholics, sex addicts, and meat eaters. It's all the same.

Akasuki used to say addiction is the manifestation of the search for higher consciousness or some shit like that. This greasy pawn shop manager is looking for Buddha by eating cake for breakfast. Who can fucking blame him? Eating cake is a decent method, and maybe it leads to enlightenment. How are we to know?

Surely it's no less legitimate than sitting on your arse, putting people in jujitsu headlocks, or stabbing them with spoons.

He offers me one hundred and fifty bucks for the Thermomix.

I thank him, head back to the car and drive up the road to *Blackhearts and Sparrows.*

The deranged pig makes its usual honk when I enter, and Meatloaf is sitting there casually swiping his phone as always. He looks up, giving me a micro nod, and quickly looks back down.

I smile naturally for a moment. He's just so damn authentic, and yet, he has no fucking clue about our history and how much he has assisted in my life to this point.

I grab two bottles of Johnnie Red because it's cheaper than the black. It's about a hundred for two bottles. I enquire about a packet of thirty Longbeach, and it's forty-two. I shake my head at the price of cigarettes and hand over the cash. Now I've got seven bucks fifty-five cents change to get a cheap fucking hot dog or some shit later.

I thank Meatloaf and tell him I'm sorry for nicking two bottles of whiskey last time, but he ignores the comment. Then I tell him I liked him in Fight Club. He barely acknowledges that one, either. No one gives a fuck anymore.

I laugh a little, then leave the shop to the pig symphony number seventeen.

I dump the cigarettes and whiskey onto the passenger seat and drive. Fuck knows where I'm going. I've decided to leave it to fate. If there is some force in the world, surely it will lead me where I need to be.

I take a huge swig of whiskey, downing about a quarter of the first bottle. It's foul peasant juice. I should have just nicked a couple of bottles of black again.

Keith's piece of shit cream Falcon drives like a dream. I'm shocked, actually, given how it looked when I first got in — the McDonald's bags and the smell of dick cheese. Maybe I caught him on a bad day — fuck knows.

Maybe he has days like mine. Maybe he has days like mine but came to fucking pick me up anyway because *that's* the method. Maybe. Fuck knows. I'm driving now and taking massive swigs from Johnnie.

I've already toked three of the thirty Longbeach.

Twenty-seven to go.

I'm thinking by the time I get to *one,* this shit will be over. It's the carcinogenic countdown. You've got to go out with a cough.

Melbourne is a beautiful city if you ignore all the damn cranes and construction pricks in their bright orange alien suits vaping like a bunch of cocks.

I press play on Keith's CD player. Given his looks, I expect seventies progressive rock like YES or RUSH. But it's some motivational CD.

— are under the impression that they have control of their minds. But when one looks closer, it is a lie. If I want a cup of coffee at the office, I will get up, make coffee and drink it, safe in the knowledge that it was 'me' that decided to drink it. Some people call it free will.

Please don't get me wrong here. I am not saying that free will does not exist. I am just saying that one won't find it where one thinks.

For our action of making and drinking coffee to be free will, one had to have the preliminary thought, 'Now I am going to think, I feel like a cup of coffee,' but since one didn't have that previous thought, the coffee thought must have arisen by itself.

Of course, such an arising cannot be random. It comes from the momentum caused by previous moments of consciousness. This cause-and-effect relationship is often known as karma. People think karma is a basic process, like universal retribution, but it isn't. Karma means that the more you head in a particular direction, the more you are likely to head in that direction in future. One can liken it to momentum. Karma can be challenging to change, like turning a ship around or trying to stop a snowball from rolling down a hill.

But that doesn't mean one cannot change it. If one never takes the time to observe the mind, then karma is left to its own devices. The actions of the past create momentum or habits, which become the winds of thought. One believes in their thought winds as self and acts upon them, such as in the example of the coffee. One drinks coffee in the past, creating momentum or habit. That is reflected as the thought, 'I feel like a cup of coffee,' which is then acted upon, creating further momentum. The more one indulges a thought, the stronger it returns due to the wind of karma or momentum.

An understanding of this process makes clear that in the essential function of the mind, there is no such thing as free will and that, under the spell of identification with thoughts, we are prisoners of our past actions.

Free will does not exist within the identification of thought but within the act of acknowledging the presence of awareness. Rather than believing one's thoughts to be oneself, one can recognise thought as the reflection of one's past actions. Suppose a practitioner can recognise thoughts as they arise. In that case, it is possible to act contrary to that thought based on a universal vision or, if one is spiritually inclined, to allow the observance of the said thought to release the pattern back upon itself.

It might be helpful to consider this notion concerning the physical bo-bo-bo-bo-bo-bo-bo-bo-bo-bo-bo-bo-bo-bo-bo-bo-bo-bo-bo-bo-bo-bo-bo-bo-bo-bo-bo-bo-bo-bo-bo-bo-bo-bo-bo-bo-bo-bo- bo-bo —

Fuck. The CD is stuck, and I've been in a trance listening to that shit. Who uses fucking CDs these days anyway?

I want to believe that it's some fate-driven sign on my path towards selflessness, but I honestly can't seem to get any meaning out of it. I realise that I know fuck all about Keith except for his days writing music for Psychedelic Cock or whatever his band was called. Yet, this is some heavy philosophy. It's the work, I suppose. It's the method.

For a second, I regret not listening at our coffee meeting. But then the feeling goes away.

The carcinogenic clock says *twenty-six* now, and Johnnie is well and truly occupying the same space as I am. I'm burning down King Street, but I slow down to look at the strip clubs getting ready for their evening of filthy action. I've never liked strip clubs, but it's not for some moral reason. It's just that standing in a room with a bunch of blokes getting a stiffy is not for me.

I drive straight over the bridge, past the murky Yarra River and the casino. I don't know where the fuck I'm going. Driving is like running in a way. As long as you're moving, there's no anxiety.

I'm calm as a Zen monk now. I've found the method. It's selfless-ness. It's the extinguishing of the self in its physical form. I'm still unclear on the exact plan, but I know it's happening tonight.

It's seven-thirty, and there's about an hour of damn optimism left in this sun. The death of the sun is the only thing that concerns me about real-time. I'm on carcinogenic time now, and that says *twenty-five* to go.

I'm waiting for sundown for several reasons. You can't go fucking killing yourself in broad daylight. There's too much damn activity. People *expect* shit to happen at night, but when it occurs during the day, it will be all over the news.

Second, I still don't know how it's going to happen. I'm waiting for a sign. I'm waiting for God or Buddha or someone to launch a giant fucking hand out of the sky and whip me across the face.

I'm driving through the lower eastern suburbs. I know where I'm going now, but I didn't want to go direct. It's too painful to go direct. I have to trick myself into getting there.

I need to stop for a piss, so I get out in a clean green park. The sun's going down, and people are sitting around with bottles of Chardonnay and biscuits and fucking cheese. They're laughing about fuck knows what. They have things to laugh about. I'm heading for the public toilet block with a quarter bottle of Johnnie and a Longbeach hanging out of my mouth.

The bog stinks like bleach. Someone must have had a wank in here. Either that or the cleaners have been. Spunk and bleach smell the same.

My piss is dark. It's the same colour as Johnnie, and I wonder if I'm pissing pure whiskey, so I dunk my hand in and take a mouthful. It tastes like piss — watery with a dry aftertaste that gives you a fucking face spasm.

I shake my cock a few times, then loosen the elastic of Astrid's white and blue stripy Bonds knickers. Then I shake again. I put my cock away, and now there's a piss stain on Astrid's purest. It's impossible to shake your cock dry after the age of thirty. We all need fucking nappies.

I consider if I need to shit, but there's no way. I haven't eaten a fucking thing all day except Anthony Weasley's forearm. The last thing I ate was a bowl of Brenda's stew last night and a piece of cake leftover from the soup kitchen that tasted like someone had used spunk as an egg replacement. It's possible, I'm sure.

The graffiti on the wall says *Pig's dick,* and I wonder what the purpose of it is as I walk out again among the lawn-based middle-class partygoers.

A few of them look at me funny, so I have to check if Astrid's knickers are showing. I realise they aren't, so I undo my pants and show them. Fuck these pricks.

"Pig's Dick," I say to one couple as I pass. Then I do it again to another.

"Pig's dick, pig's dick!" I yell.

I don't know why I'm doing it. That's what a bottle of scotch will do for you. It makes sense because it doesn't.

The bottle is empty now, and I'm smoking another Longbeach.

Twenty-three.

I get back in the Falcon and take a deep breath. The sky has turned to a pale shade of sudsy pink with mildly aquamarine flecks.

I start the car and screech up the road, past the pub-goers drinking their espresso martinis, laughing about their investments, stocks, and shares and why Miffy's husband had an affair with the cleaner Margherita.

It's sickening. I hate them. But it's not their fault. I hate them because I *was* one of them. What was the purpose of it all? What is the purpose of any of it?

It comes. It fucking goes. *That's it.*

Akasuki used to say that death is the hardest meditation object but also the most important. He was right about that. I've thought about it a lot.

Twenty-one.

I'm driving up my old street now, opposite my old house. I pull up and turn off the creamy engine. It's quiet except for those fucking crickets and the barely audible sound of money.

I forgot how beautiful this street was. There are lampposts and trees — something you never fucking see in the West. There's also a lack of silver paint sniffers here — only refined, stuck-up white capitalist middle-class pigs and wealthy Chinese. And go on — tell me why that's wrong, you fucker. You might have to think about it for a while.

Twenty

I've cracked the second bottle of Johnnie and drunk at least ten per cent of it. I head over to the fence and hold tight, gazing into my past.

I know I'm supposed to say something poetic like *it's the fucking grey shadow of my dreams* or some shit but fuck you. It's not like that. It's just shit — negative fucking dark, black shit, so fuck you.

I can see him — my dog. He is in the garden wagging his tail like a maniac at the gate because I'm coming home — the only one who ever loved me unconditionally. He *lived* for me. He lived for our life, and it fucking burns. It's molten lead. *Fuck.* I want to kiss him, hold him and tell him it's all going to be alright. He wouldn't understand, but he wouldn't care. He just wanted me to *be* there, and I wasn't. Now he's gone. And my face is wet with fucking bad, bad tears, and my stomach is wet with dark, dark whiskey.

I'm feeling dizzy and fucking drunk. The house is dark and empty, but I imagine a light on in the kitchen, and she's there watching some tv show on the food channel and following along, making a damn masterpiece dinner for me.

I'm upstairs in the second room from the left, looking at a fucking Excel spreadsheet, waiting for her to shout up to me,

Do you want to come and eat down here?

So I can say,

No thanks. I don't have time. Can you bring it up?

You twat. You stupid, stupid twat.

Fuck. I rattle the fence and shout unintelligible syllables at the crickets. Those *fuckers*.

I'm weeping and bawling like a fucking animal and pissing snot and saliva all over the pavement and then coughing and coughing and dry reaching. I turn round to kick the tree, but I miss and fall backwards into the gutter, smashing my head on the pavement. But I'm not dead. I'm not even bleeding, damn it.

At least I saved the bottle. I perch myself against the tree and take a few slugs. Then I pull a Longbeach out of the packet and light it.

Nineteen

I should start thinking about the schedule. And I should get out of here before some fucker calls the cops. The last thing I need is a night in a cell. I've got work to do.

I pull myself up and stumble back to the Falcon. I get in and start the engine, taking one last look back at our place — my dog wagging his tail at the gate, waiting for me — my wife eating dinner *without* me. Then I stick my middle finger up at the useless prick on the computer upstairs and screech off.

Eighteen

I should have researched this better. If I'm honest, I have no fucking idea how to commit suicide. I'd heard from people in the gaff that a shotgun under the chin is the most effective, aka most likely to kill you instantly.

I'm down for that shit. But where can you find a shotgun on a Friday night? This isn't South Central Los Angeles. You can't just walk up to some schmunk in the street and buy a machine gun. You can't just walk into Walmart and purchase a semi-automatic with five hundred rounds and some ear defenders to go with your cornflakes and salt n vinegar chips.

I don't know. Maybe you can't even do that in America anymore, but this is Australia. Prime Minister John Howard, AKA Mr Sheen, banned semi-automatics years ago after that prick Bryant shot up all those people in Tasmania.

Seventeen

I'm sure people thought he was just being a prick — Bryant, that is — but it's never that simple. Humans are complex. That bastard probably had some kind of logic for the whole thing that would have made sense to him at the time.

I'm not excusing what he did. I'm just saying that I know how quickly a thought can gain power and start to rule you —especially thoughts you *don't want* to have. The more you try and push them away, the more they dominate you.

One minute you're alright. The next, you're thinking of raping someone or stabbing them in the neck with a spoon, or you've shot up a bunch of innocent tourists.

We're all just one car crash away from fucking a miniature horse.

Sixteen

I'm two-thirds down this next bottle of Johnnie, and I know I'm intoxicated because I'm swerving all over the road. I've always been quite a skilled drunk driver, but I don't know many people who follow road rules after 1.75 bottles of Johnnie Red.

It's not going to be enough to kill me. I'd need at least one more bottle and maybe some pills. I feel sick as fuck, but I'm fighting the urge to blow this devil's liquid back up and all over Keith's damn car.

I think about Keith for a minute. The bastard's probably gone to make dinner for everyone and realised his Thermomix has gone. Maybe he's even realised his car has gone. Maybe he's called the damn cops. Maybe they've put an APB out on me, whatever the fuck that means.

All units, we have an APB on a Nick Conrad. The suspect is five feet ten inches tall, driving a stolen shit cream Falcon and wearing a cocaine shirt, tight pants, and stolen women's panties.

For a minute, I feel bad. Keith, that skinny, greasy speedhead bastard, was always nice to me. I think about calling him but quickly realise I smashed the phone he gave me.

Fifteen

I need to get back on point. These diversions are a waste of time. So, I drive and drive and plot and think. I should have planned this better. The old me would have. I would have scheduled it step by step in some Gantt chart, then white boarded it and done some PowerPoint presentation for the stakeholders — at present, that's Johnnie and me. But not the new me. I'm no project manager of death. I'm a Zen master on a dry mission to find selflessness. I'm attempting the ultimate ego death — the death of the body.

Akasuki used to say that suicide is an extreme risk to someone with mental pain because there's no proof that the mind doesn't continue after death. What would he know? He isn't even Asian. How can he be enlightened?

Fourteen

I'm staring at a vast, perfect white moon and waiting for a sign. It's honestly the biggest moon I've ever seen. And I know I should recite a spontaneous spiritual poem as any decent Zen master would, but I can't think of anything to say about the big white round bastard, so fuck it.

"Excuse me, Mate?" It's one of those bastard window washers. Usually, I'd ignore the prick, but washing Keith's window is the least I can offer the greasy skunk for stealing his car and Thermomix.

He looks like Tim Minchin on heroin. I give him my best drunken nineteen eighties thumbs up. He grins like an ecstatic toad and cleans my window like he is wanking off the Queen.

I have seven dollars and fifty-five cents. I was going to get a hot dog, but it's too late now. There are no hot dogs in Nirvana. As Akasuki would say, how could there be since hot dogs are conditioned phenomena?

I open the now shabby Longbeach box and count them. There are twelve and two snapped ones. I grab two good ones, the two snapped ones and add them to the pile of change, which I pour into the man's hands like I'm filling his bowl with soup. He smiles at me like I just gave him a rim job with all the trimmings, and he cries.

I reach out and hold his hand. And for a second, I feel something. I don't know what this feeling is. It could be the booze, but it feels like *connection*, and I also cry.

There's just me and this crazy window bastard standing in the middle of these cash-soaked streets bawling over a few bucks and a few ciggies.

Two mad fannies.

"Fucking Pig's dick," I say, and he laughs his bollocks off.

"Sorry," I say. "I don't know why I said that."

Again, it could be the booze, but this feels like *the* moment. It feels like the moon reaching out and asking me if I'm serious like I'm a potential Zen student sitting outside the temple in the pissing rain for three weeks.

"Look, Mate," I say. "This might sound strange, but would you know the best way someone could commit suicide?"

The light's gone green, and a Hyundai Getz is beeping behind me. But that fucker can wait.

Minchin gets a serious look on his face.

"Ya see that building there," he says, nodding and pointing up at a huge, half-finished building with the bright moon above it.

"Yes,"

"It's a construction site, but you can easily get up there. There are steps all the way up. It's easy to get in. Go to the top and jump off it. This time of night, there'll be no one around."

I'm a little shocked at his straight-up advice like I asked him for directions to the Seven-Eleven.

The Hyundai driver spins around me and stops for a moment.

"You *arsehole*," he yells.

Any other day, I would relish the opportunity to climb out of my car and kick the fucker's tiny windshield in, but not today. I smile peacefully, and he fucks off.

"Thanks, man," I say, gripping the window washer's hands tightly and tearing up again. There was no advice, no conditioned pushing me toward the light or asking me *why* — only respect for the method.

"You sound like an expert," I say as he scratches at the last bit of birdshit with his fingernail.

"I am," he says. "I've thought about it a lot, Man, so I've analysed all the options. Course, there's always a risk of survival with any method, but that's high enough to give you at least a 96.2% chance of getting it right."

I bow mentally to him.

"Good luck, Man," he says.

I drive off slowly with a lump in my throat. That was *something*. For a moment, I consider calling the whole damn thing off, but I've come too far. The Buddha would surely not approve of my inability to follow through with this commitment. He would probably beat me with his shoe, and I would fall unconscious and wake up, realising I was the Buddha and the whole time I had been beating myself up.

I light up another Longbeach and reach over to check out the status of the carcinogenic clock.

There's *nine*. No, make that *eight*.

I pull up out the front of the half-finished skyscraper and stare up at the giant white sphere in the sky.

"*Always shoot for the moon,*" I say to myself. I don't know why. It's just one of those drunken phrases.

I sit and smoke another two Longbeach. My throat's fucking sore. I could use some water, but there's probably no need. Still, I don't want to die thirsty. Akasuki said we need to die in a calm state of mind. I'm reasonably calm, but I don't want to die wishing I had water and get reborn as a damn fish in an aquarium.

I've got no money to buy a big chunk of plastic wrapped around a tiny bit of water. I've got an empty whiskey bottle, though, and there's bound to be a tap somewhere. Capitalism has its benefits — as short-lived as they may come to be.

I find a tap down the side of the building, fill up the Johnnie bottle and drink some. It tastes like chemicals from a factory.

Now I'm breaking into this construction site like a teenager finding a place to smoke oregano. I rip off the board that leads to the stairs, and I fall back like a twat on my arse once again. I lie there for a minute and notice the sky and the stars, and I remember I'm on this floating ball of capitalism in space.

Space — the final frontier. What the fuck does that mean anyway? I take a Longbeach lying on my back and explore space for a minute like Captain Twirk — boldly going where — hmm —

Eight! I shout. Then I double-check. *Seven*, I whisper. The countdown is getting low.

Am I going to go through with this? I know that's what *you're* thinking. You think this is one of those cries for help. Even at this point in the story, you don't know me well at all. I've shared everything with you, you fucker. I've even talked about my *transgressive* thoughts, and in this day and age, that's the kind of shit that can get you strung up like an old chorizo.

I'm not George Costanza on top of Pretty Woman in Pretty Woman. I didn't need Richard Gere to drag me off. I'm George, *and* I'm Richard. I dragged *myself* off.

These thoughts just come. You don't choose them. Your thought is a reflection of the past. That's what Keith's CD said, I think.

It's what Akasuki used to say as well. Thoughts aren't who we are. They are who we *used* to be. By identifying with them, we make them our future also. Ego is like the gaffer tape that ties the past and future together. Fuck, maybe that CD did make sense.

So, if I'm telling you about my thoughts, I trust you enough to listen, so don't try to fuck my life, okay?

Sorry for going off at you. I appreciate you being here. It's the sky that's stressful. It's the white moon and the stars, those fuckers. It's not all the other shit.

I pull myself up slowly. I'm at whiskey level 92.67 now, and I'm smushing myself through a six-inch gap between the concrete and the wood because, at some level, I think I'm still sixteen and skinny as fuck and able to leap tall buildings in a single bound — or leap *off* them.

It's dark in here. This is the kind of situation where a light would be helpful — maybe a phone. It would be good if it weren't in pieces back in Keith's bin, along with those Johnnie bottles.

I try to light my lighter for a bit, but I get about fourteen concrete steps high before the bastard burns the inside of my thumb, and I drop the fucker.

It takes me what seems like an hour to find it in the dark again. I take another big swig of Johnnie, but I swallow and remember it's just fucking water, so I smash it against the wall in a tantrum and then remember I'm fucking thirsty.

It's dark, obviously, and I can't see shit. I light up two Longbeach at once to give me a better view and to help me get to the end of this carcinogenic countdown quicker. But the dim red hue barely helps at all. Where's Carol Vorderman when you need her? And, how many tickers are left on this waster clock? Is it *four* or *five* or something?

I've covered another thirty to forty steps, and my drunken eyes are finally adjusting to the darkness. I'm sweating like a nervous lizard, and it's gone from pitch black to hazy blue.

I expected to emerge in glory through some door onto a roof like it's the Matrix, but I can see now that this roof is barely fixed, and the final steps give way into some fucking disaster zone full of hazards. It's a health and safety nightmare. Someone could get hurt up here.

On top of that, it's damn windy, and I'm wondering if I'll even need to leap or if Mother Nature might do the job for me by blowing me off herself.

I stumble across metal pipes, rods, and concrete blocks and whack my shins repeatedly. I'm pretty sure I'm bleeding now as I circle the roof looking for a place to settle in for a ciggie. I find a lovely spot on top of a solid concrete block with a few choice chips out of it and a couple of rusty rods sticking up for me to hold onto, and I settle in.

The concrete's cold and feels good on my arse, which is hot from walking up many steps. I estimate I'm on floor thirty or some shit. All

I know is it's fucking high, and the view is exceptional in all directions — especially the moon.

I owe a lot to that window washer. Who could have known such a beautiful view was so close by?

Melbourne is full of hidden gems like this. That's what they say in all those lifestyle magazines, anyway. There are hidden coffee bars under the seats of public lavatories and taco bars where the plates are made from the used syringes of dead junkies, that kind of thing.

You could probably turn this construction site into a bar or restaurant — the sort of place where you put on a hard hat and hi-vis vest before you sit down to enjoy a hi-altitude plate of yuzu-marinated antelope cock with a side of wilted spinach that's been passed through a badger's arsehole —not that they have badgers in Australia. Let's make it a platypus or a wallaby or a crocodile hunter with corks hanging from his hat and dead possum shoes and —

Fuck it. For a minute there, I was feeling better, and I just can't let that happen. It's selfish to feel good. Feeling good equals shame. Selflessness is the method, and we're here for one thing and one thing only — to overcome attachment to this physical manifestation of ego and desire.

I shuffle up to the edge of the block and light up a Longbeach. I dangle my legs off the sheer drop and suck in the blue smoke, blowing it out into the wind-ripped sky.

The wind calms down like it received my smoke offering and the message of my intention. It's weirdly calm up here all of a sudden, and it feels like the whole universe is chanting my name and beckoning me to jump into the void.

Con—rad, Con—rad, Con—rad.

I'm perched on the edge of this life and the afterlife, and I'm briefly grateful for the experience. How many people get to do this? I should have brought a notebook to document the experience on the way down.

Dear Diary

I'm falling at approximately forty-two miles per hour. I aim to hit the obligatory eighty-eight miles per hour before the flux capacitor in the head of my cock fires out green flames, and I'm transported into Hill Valley in 1955. The aim is to splatter this wasted corpse on the pavement below at maximum speed and preferably head first to ensure a terrific exit from this damned world. Now I'm halfway down, do I regret my decision? Absolutely I do. But isn't life just a series of painful regrets? Also, it's cold. They never tell you how cold it is jumping off buildings. I should have done more research. After all, it's the middle of summer. Who would have expected this? I could catch a death of cold at this rate. I should've worn a jumper. Now, I'm on my back looking upwards, and I'm not sure this is the best way to fall. I could shatter my spine and every bone in my body, but my head hits an old goon bag, a passing hedgehog, an abandoned colostomy bag, or a balloon, which saves only my head. I could end up like that wizard Steven Hawkeye wandering around in a moveable chair with a robot voice. Would that be so bad? I don't know.

It's raining now — not in the diary, but here in so-called real life. I've always preferred rain. Rain is melancholy soup. It forces you to drink in your immortality and — *Jesus Christ, am I stalling here?* I'm harping on like that bastard Shakespeare or someone. Get on with it already, you fanny.

Drinking two bottles of Johnnie is a mixed blessing. It gives you the bollocks to consider throwing yourself off a building, but it also makes the pain bearable. And now, I try to think of my wife or dog to bring on the tears, but it's not happening. I can't see a reason to throw myself off. I've ruined the job.

Prior Preparation and Planning Prevent Piss Poor Performance — the seven Ps. That's what they teach young pricks who want to be successful. It's nonsense, of course, and this isn't about me anyway. It's about the method — it's about selflessness. I have to do this.

I shuffle forward a touch more. One single push forward, and it's game on. Why am I doing this, though? That's the question.

It's fine. People commit suicide all the time. But maybe the goal is *killing* me. Excuse the pun. It's that fear of failure thing. When the goal is too big, the fear of failure inevitably leads to failure because the only way to succeed is to risk massive failure.

I don't know where I got that. Maybe it came from Keith's CD in his car or some podcast from the past. Still, to fail, you need *something* to fail at, and I have nothing.

Anyway, fuck it. Here we go. I'm Neo. Morpheus is behind me. All I have to do is free my mind. Free. My. Mind.

Fuck, this is harder than I thought. Just jump, you bastard. I might need to run up like Neo. Maybe if I just —

FUCK ME.

There's a dark figure behind me, and I nearly throw myself off to escape its clutches.

"Fuck you, Batman," I say. Then I wonder if I have already jumped. Maybe these are the hallucinations of the afterlife, and this is the grim reaper come to reap whatever results I have sown during this wast—

"Hello, Nicholas," says a soft but terrifying voice. It lacks the deep-throaty, growl of Bale's Batman. It sounds slightly Transylvanian instead. It sounds just like —

"Lunchmore?" I say.

The gothic bloodsucker steps forward, showing himself, soaked from the rain and panting, having climbed mountains of steps or flying up here with his giant flappy bat wings, which are now revealed as a yellow poncho like the type they wear at tennis matches in the rain.

"I mean, what the fuck? What the fuck are you? How? How did you?"

"Astrid told me," he says, stepping forward again.

Damn it. I forgot about Astrid. How could I forget she existed? She is the love of my — no, no, she isn't. I forgot about her, so how could she be? She must have been aware of everything that's happened so far and has done nothing to —

"I wonder why she didn't come and get me?" I say to Lunchmore.

"Nicholas, I'm here for two reasons," he says, stepping forward again.

"Don't come any closer, Lunchmore," I say.

He does that *okay, okay* thing like he doesn't want me to jump.

"I'm not going to jump. I just don't want you to fucking bite me again."

"Yes, sorry about that, Nicholas. Did you say you're *not* going to jump?"

"No, well, yes, maybe. I don't know."

"I'm not going to bite you, Nicholas," he says, laughing. It's the first time I've seen him laugh.

"I had no idea you were capable of emotion," I say to him, and he laughs some more.

"I'll just sit here," he says. Now his face goes even sterner than before, like the use of his laughter energy forced him deeper into the grim.

"I'm here for two reasons, Nicholas," he says again. "It's like killing two birds with one stone if you'll excuse the rather insensitive pun." He smiles again, just slightly this time. It seems we are both into the death puns this evening.

"Firstly, of course, Astrid knew what was happening to you. She told me she felt like you needed it but that I was to come and find you at this exact location and time."

I shuffle a little further away from the edge and sit on a block adjacent to Lunchmore's block, cracking my tailbone on another rusty rod.

There's water running down his face from the rain, but I swear he is crying.

"Are you crying, Lunchmore?" I ask in an insensitive, belittling tone. I didn't mean that.

"As it happens," he says, struggling with his words, "There's *another* reason why I'm here."

"Okay," I say. It's getting cold now. I wish he would get to the point.

"It's Keith," he says.

"What about Keith?" I say. "Is he coming after me with a bolt gun for stealing his Thermomix?"

"What? No," Lunchmore says. "Keith had a heart attack this afternoon at the soup kitchen, Nicholas."

The blood leaves my face and leaps off the edge of the building, and tears fill my eyes. Now I'm suddenly getting vertigo.

What the fuck are we doing on top of this building?

"Is he okay?" I ask. I know the answer.

Lunchmore hangs his head for a moment, then looks at me again.

"He *passed away* at Footscray Hospital, Nicholas. They tried to revive him but said it was a massive heart attack and he would have left immediately."

Even Johnnie can't stop the next wave of grief. It comes from my belly in deep pulses. Tears are mixing with rain and hitting the concrete.

I don't know why, but I'm hanging my head and physically crying now. So much for the booze numbing the pain. I wish I was sober for this. Why do I even care about the stupid skinny, speed head wet ferret fuck?

I feel an arm around me. It's Lunchmore. He looks like a gothic Tony Bennett. He looks at me and nods, then he holds me. No biting, just compassion. It feels like back at the Zen temple with Brenda and Berthandra.

I cry and cry, and I can see that he is too. It's the weirdest thing in the world, just myself and the man who tried to eat me, on top of a building site, thirty storeys up, in the pissing rain.

It's a moment. And I feel, for a second, that this is it. *This* is life.

It's not just the pleasure. It's the madness and the pain. But the pain is okay when it's shared with others. We're meant to grieve *together*. Not alone.

Fuck me. I'm shitting on like Shakespeare again. We need to get off this fucking rooftop.

"We need to get off this rooftop," I say.

"Come on, Nicholas," says Lunchmore. "I'll buy you a hot dog."

The Ghosts Of Superheroes

I t's like Pulp Fiction for meth heads.

We walk into the diner, soaked to the skin — Lunchmore with his pale Transylvanian face in his yellow tennis poncho and me, drunk, red-eyed in my cocaine shirt, which is now transparent and displaying my hairy nipples.

People shuffle in their seats awkwardly. I've been getting used to that. I remember for a minute telling the Zen student to go fuck himself, and I laugh out loud, not because it's funny but because I understand where he was coming from.

You get so lost in your anarchy sometimes that you think people are being arseholes. You don't realise that you're the arsehole, and they're displaying *courage* by stepping out of line and confronting you.

I want someone to do that to us now — stand up and say, *well, will you look at these two nutjobs*, like it's an old coffee shack in backyard America or something. I wouldn't get aggressive, I don't think. I'd probably join in with the self belittling.

"Hi, Steve," says one of the waitresses. I look around to see if there's another customer behind us.

"Hi, Maggie," says Lunchmore.

"Usual table?" she asks.

He nods, and we sit in a delicate oxblood booth by the window with cracked seats. It's soft and comfortable as I drip rain onto the laminated menu from my hair.

"Order whatever you want, Nicholas. It's on me," says Lunchmore.

"Thanks, *Steve*," I say teasingly, but he doesn't react.

Why would he? His name's Steve, and when you think about it, there's nothing weird about that. I suppose only myself and others built up the Count Lunchmore persona.

He pulls off his Bananaman cape to reveal an old-looking green sweater with a name badge that says *Lonschmoor*.

I stare at it for a second as I feel my ideas of him dissolving rapidly.

"Can I get you gentlemen any coffees to start?" says the waitress, a thirty-something brunette with giant pink hoop earrings.

"Yes, I'll get a long black. Thanks, Maggie. Nicholas? How about you?"

"I'll get the same, thanks," I say.

Maggie shuffles off, and Steve Lonschmoor sits analysing the plastic menu for a minute.

"I think I'm going to have the Dirk Diggler," he says.

I check out the list of hot dogs on the back of the menu. They're all named after famous porn stars.

I feel strangely calm in Steve's presence. The summer rain hits the window outside again, and it's like that famous picture where all the dead celebrities — Monroe, Dean and the rest — are sitting in the late-night diner.

I think about Keith again and how much I ignored his communication. I just sat there thinking about my own shit like a loser. I immediately judged him like I judged Steve Lonschmoor.

And yeah, I know, it's a hell of a transformation for an hour or so. But don't worry. It's temporary. You'll be surprised how much the intention of death and high altitude rain and the shock of seeing Batman and the death of someone you know and the remembrance of the one you love and a massive hug, not to mention two bottles of Johnnie can change you, even if it is just for the rest of the night.

The waitress brings over our coffees.

Lonschmoor orders the Dirk Diggler. I get a plain hot dog with cheese and sweet potato fries. It's the first time I've ordered bread in a while, and I'm okay with it. It feels normal to order hot dogs. I like normal tonight.

I think of the window washer and wish he was here. I'd ask Lonschmoor to buy him a hot dog and a coffee.

"So, were you and Keith close then?" I ask.

Surely it's better than the *how did you know Keith?* common icebreaker question.

Lonschmoor takes a sip of his coffee and leans back in his chair.

"We served together in Afghanistan," he says.

For a second, I think he's joking. It's the kind of thing I would say for a joke. But he isn't joking.

I suddenly notice a look of strength in Lonschmoor's eyes and feel the respect welling up in my bones — it's a certain degree of awe when you meet someone who's been to war. I can't think of what to ask next, but I sense it's not the time for me to speak but to listen anyway.

"Keith was my commanding officer, you see," he says. "He was a captain and a *fearless* man. I was his sergeant."

"I would have thought it was the other way around," I say rudely. Lonschmoor smiles kindly.

"Most people do. We're both very different people now," he says.

"I feel bad for stressing Keith out like maybe I contributed to his —passing," I say, making everything about myself as usual and interrupting the flow of Steve's story.

"Don't be absurd, Nicholas," he says, getting slightly irritated. "It was first and foremost the amphetamines he consumed every waking hour, not to mention his horrific lifestyle. It had nothing to do with you whatsoever."

It's a tremendously kind thing to say. I see the method in this man. He's no vampire. He's a saint — maybe. I've still witnessed his ability to dig his teeth in and —

"Anyway," I say, pulling myself back out of my head and into the diner. "Thanks for saying that. I'm sorry for interrupting Steve. You were saying about how you met in the army."

The waitress returns with our hot dogs and puts the wrong ones in front of each of us and sweet potato fries with aioli in the middle. I grab a handful of chips and stuff them into my gob.

"Keith saved my life on more than one occasion," he says, swapping the plates. "There was one particular day I won't talk about just now. It probably led, in large part, to the flaws that both of us carry — *carried* around."

I take a massive bite of hot dog and feel the hiccups coming. It happens when I eat bread. It could be a stress reaction, but I don't think so. It has happened since long before the crap hit the pan.

I start hiccuping rapidly, and it feels like I'm ruining the vibe.

Steve stops his story and pours me a glass of water which instantly cures my hiccups. Then he continues to ignore his food and talk.

"During that time, I had an enemy soldier on top of me," he says. "He was just a young bloke — probably nineteen or twenty. I noticed his tattoo the most. It was a picture of a cuckoo, and under it were the words —

> *I hear the song*
> *Of cuckoo answering cuckoo all day long;*
> *And know not if it be my inward sprite*
> *For my delight*

I've inhaled my giant hot dog like Joey Chestnut, and I'm still stuffing chips into my mouth. And it probably seems like I don't care about the story, but I do. I'm just as hungry as a damn bear.

"Sorry, Steve," I say. "I'm listening. I'm just as hungry as a damn bear."

He calls the waitress over and says,

"He'll have the same again."

I remember my insight at the therapist's office that I like people because they give me things because I feel the swell of love for Lonschmoor. But I know it can't be *just* the hot dogs.

It's fucking cliché, but I feel my energy coming back, almost like Keith has passed his life force onto me. But fuck it, I know it's just for tonight. Tomorrow I'll be the same selfish prick I've always been, I'm sure. But maybe not. Anyway, it doesn't matter. It's tonight. We only have the *now*. That's what Akasuki would have said. And I'm sure Brenda's teacher said something about that as well.

"Thank you," I say to Steve.

He takes a bite of his hot dog and nods in approval at the flavour. He has ketchup down the side of his mouth, and for a moment, it reminds me of what he looked like when I was smashing his head into the Bain Marie, but I don't share this with him.

He wipes his mouth, forcing me to forget about it immediately.

"The thing was —" he continues, still chewing on the hot dog, "This kid was Afghan, and that's an *English* poem by John Swinnerton Phillimore. But the word's stuck with me. Anyway, the kid wouldn't let up. He had a bayonet in my gut, so I had no choice but to bite out his windpipe."

I've stopped stuffing fries into my mouth. I'm just sipping black coffee with a scowl on my face.

"He was just a kid, Nicholas, you know?"

I don't know what to say, so I sigh and sip more coffee.

"That's why I got the nickname *Count Lonschmoor*. I became known as the man who bit out a boy's throat. It hurt a lot, Nicholas, and one day I just snapped and bit a chunk out of a colleague's face for calling me it. The only person that didn't call me that name was Keith. Later, ironically, I got a blood disease, so I had to leave the army. And, like you, I got into all kinds of trouble with drink, drugs, and violence. I was in and out of prison for assault."

My new hot dog has arrived, and I'm not hungry. Instead, I keep filling my glass with more water to flush out the litre and a half of whiskey, trying to squeeze its way through my pickled liver.

"Later, when Keith left the army, he invited me to live with him, and we set up the soup kitchen together. But an old corporal recognised me and called me *The Count*, and the name stuck. Of course, my biting didn't help the cause."

"You and Keith started the soup kitchen *together*?"

"Yes."

"That's surprising. You know the way you talk to each other and your aggression and —"

"I know. It *is* surprising. It's a hangover from our army days, but I can assure you it's all *love*. He knows when I start to go, I start to go, and I made him promise he would *always* take me down. So, the others learned to grab me and give me a shot because I have severe anger issues. You probably shouldn't even be sitting with me now. One wrong word, and I'll try to kill you."

He has an unnerving look in his eyes.

"What about Astrid? Did she know?" I ask.

"Well, I never thought so. She hasn't been with us very long, you see. But after tonight, I'm assuming she probably knows *everything*. About a week ago, she told me I had to get used to the nickname to get over it. Then when I stopped reacting, the name would dissolve. And she's probably right. Still, it depends on the day. You got me on a bad day, Nicholas. I'm sorry about that."

He nods at me. I nod back, and for the next fifteen minutes, we sit and eat our hot dogs, watch the rain battering against the window and talk into the night like empty ghosts at their 1993 summer reunion.

I've got a serious headache now. The adrenaline has ceased to hold off that old drunken, washed-out sensation, and my depression is kicking back in hard. I feel the anxiety coming back.

I know this is where there's supposed to be some resolution and character transformation, but it's just not there. Sure, Keith is dead, but it's not enough. People die every day, nay, every damn *second*.

I'm starting to think I should have dived into the abyss when I had the chance. A hot dog with a veteran vampire isn't going to change much for me. Like I said, the next day everything's back, only the next day is coming early.

Steve senses what's happening, I think. He pays the bill, and we head out to the cream falcon. He drives me home, and I manage a greyed-out thanks and a brief handshake before shuffling up the path to the red brick entrance.

As I pass the deadly bush, I think about the first day I met Keith — when he picked me up, gave me cigarettes, and assured me everything would be okay. Then he let me into his house and gave me a room.

Happy Liberation Day, he had told me. But liberation from what? I'm beginning to understand why people re-offend to get back into the gaff. There's a numbness to it. There's a sense that you don't have to deal with things even though you do. I mean, you have a routine, and there's work, and there's a hierarchy, and you usually have what someone else wants, and that makes for a simple version of capitalism and — *fuck.*

I've had enough of this night.

There's a key under the rug where it always is, and I shuffle into the quiet house. I flick on the light in the kitchen and stare for a minute at the empty spot where the Thermomix should be. I fall into a kitchen chair and stare at the space between the jars of cooking herbs and the microwave. There's just a damn space now.

It's like Keith's life. Between the soup kitchen and the shit-cream Falcon, there's just a damn space. No explanation. No apologies. Just space.

I grab one of the cloudy old pint glasses from the cupboard and fill it with chemical water from the old metal taps.

The moon is shining from the kitchen window. No explanation. No apologies. *Just moon.* I wish I could make it mean something — some sedative that makes it okay to be alive and full of all these thoughts.

It's like when people say our loved ones never leave us and that we are never really separate. Whole religions are based around that sedative, but it's not enough. You can't just hear those words. You also have to be sucked in enough to believe them. That belief is like the frosting on the window that hides your pain. In reality, death is truly fucked. Can there be anything more painful? It's like the ultimate kick in the gonads.

I open the fridge. It's not like I'm hungry. If anything, I'm bloated from pornstar hot dogs and sweet, sweet potato fries, but I need to distract myself from the rise of depression that's occurring.

The fridge is a typical human one. There are forty-seven types of condiments, from the fermented mouse dicks to the eight-year-old darkened sriracha sauce to the pickled white shit at the back with the faded label. There's milk, but it's old. I can tell because it's got that white crusty shit clinging to the side of the plastic bottle.

I close the fridge and make my way into Astrid's room, half expecting her to be lying in bed, but she isn't. It's humid in there, but it's clean, and there are fresh sheets on the bed, and a note, which I assume must be from her.

It isn't. It's from Keith.

Nicky, My Man

I hope you are doing alright today.

I want you to know that I understand why you are reluctant to help with everything. If I'm honest, I would probably feel that same way myself. I've been where you are, my Son. It's not the same, but I think I understand. Just know that I'm here to help you with whatever you need.

All the best, Pal

Keith

Only he isn't here. He's gone. There's just a fucking space and all that. And yeah, I know I'm expected to cry again here, but I'm not going to. I'm too dry. The booze has soaked it all up.

I'm tired, so I flick the light off and climb into Astrid's bed.

I think about Astrid and wonder what she's up to, and I sing *Patience* by *Guns N' Roses* for no reason.

All we need is just a little patience.

Fuck.

Now I'm fucking crying.

There *was* a bit left.

Black And Gold

I wake up in Astrid's bed.

The sun offers me three rays of its finest, and I'm happy to take them. I owe the sun an apology. I don't hate it today.

I get up, look through Astrid's underwear drawer and find a black pair in honour of Keith.

I walk through the house, past the blank space where the Thermomix should have been. Then, I go and sit on the back step in the warmth. I reach into my top pocket and find the Longbeach packet. There are *two* left. And I light *one* of them.

"He cared for you, you know?" comes a voice from behind. It's Brenda.

She sits down and puts her arm around me. Then she looks at me and smiles.

"It's hard to know that at the beginning because there's too much going on. But eventually, you see it. Or, you would have."

I say nothing.

"How's your hangover, Nick?" she says.

I still say nothing. I've lost the ability to speak. Somebody died last night, and it wasn't me, and that doesn't make any sense at all.

"I'm sorry," I say.

First, I'm sorry for not speaking.

She squeezes my hand, and the tears come, slowly at first.

I soon realise I'm sorry for my thoughts, my actions toward her group, and my desire to harm her. Then I realise I'm apologising to Keith.

The tears flow hard, and my throat cramps.

I'm sorry for not seeing what he did for me. I'm sorry for taking the piss out of his appearance. I'm sorry for stealing the Thermomix and the car.

"Most of all, I'm sorry for not helping out with the soup kitchen."

I realise I've said this last bit out loud.

"It's okay, love." Brenda hugs me intensely, like my mother. And that's what she feels like now. "It's not too late, you know?" she says. She's right about that.

I finish my Longbeach, return to the lounge and pull Keith's whiteboard from behind the couch. It still has his diagram of how to shave balls correctly.

Andrew comes in, sees it, and laughs. Then we both laugh.

I turn the board over and draw new diagrams about how we can reorganise the meditation retreat to maximise profit, but I'm not back in the East ignoring anyone. I'm looking Andrew and Brenda directly in the eyes. I'm with them as I speak. I'm never going to ignore them again.

They need me now, and I need them. We all need each other. We're —

Alright, alright, I know it's a bit over the top, but that's what happens. We fling from one extreme to another. Maybe I'm bipolar. Maybe I'm — well, it doesn't matter anyway.

I open up my knowledge, and over the next two days, we reorganise the retreat so it will make enough money to save the soup kitchen with some spare change left over to cover Keith's funeral.

◆

I don't mind funerals. There's usually decent food and free booze. Everyone wears black, which limits the opportunity for rambunctious fashion choices. And sure, it's a chance for religious people to be fundamentalists, but fuck it. It's a small price to pay for good sandwiches and *whore*-derves.

I'm wearing a tight, faded black jacket and Kmart shirt I found in Keith's wardrobe. Is it weird to wear a dead man's clothes to his funeral? Perhaps, but I don't give a fuck. It's not like he needs them anymore. They'll no doubt bury him in a ten thousand dollar CK suit. That's what they do. People look far fancier in death than they do in life.

I'm in the kitchen drinking coffee with Brenda and Andrew when an immaculate soldier in a dark green beret and a chest full of medals enters the room. My jaw almost hits the cheap linoleum floor when I see him. It's Sergeant Steve Lonschmoor — *war hero.* I can't find any words, but tears fill my eyes, and I nod at him. It's all I can manage.

He nods back.

"Nicholas," he says, and his voice makes my hair stand on end.

I feel the urge to stand up straight, stop my damn slouching and brush my hair and shave and polish my damn boots.

Brenda steps up next to Steve and straightens his tie, which is already straighter than a straight man's ruler.

We all look at each other because we know she *needs* to do it anyway.

Tears are pouring down Brenda's face, so Steve pulls her in tight and holds her for a minute while Andrew and I bow our heads respectfully.

Respect — it's something you lose when you are trapped by your internal dialogue. I want to go and find the noseless man at Footscray station, the window washer, the guys at the Zen centre and Akasuki, the Western Zen teacher. I want to bow to them, touch my head to the ground three times like De La Soul and tell them I see them all.

We take the cream Falcon to the church. Steve is driving with Brenda in the passenger seat, and Andrew and I sit in the back.

Brenda talks about using too much flour in the carrot cake she baked for the usual post-funeral food show. She keeps saying she should have stuck with her standard recipe but wanted to deal with the excessive moisture that had plagued her recent carrot cake attempts.

I look across at her and smile a lips together, moon smile. It's the kind of smile that says, *no-one gives a fuck about the cake Brenda but keep talking anyway because we all know it's how you are dealing with the grief.*

People deal with their grief in very different ways.

Brenda likes to talk and straighten ties.

Sergeant Lonschmoor drives on, unaware of my frequent glances of admiration.

Andrew scrolls through his phone.

"Have you tried using an extra egg, Brenda?" says Lonschmoor.

Andrew and I look up in surprise. I think we both thought he was locked into driving, but it seems he was present with Brenda as well.

This is where I usually start ranting about the method again, but not today. Today is about Keith, not me. Perhaps that *is* the method, but I'm not going to talk about it being the method because that kills the method.

It *has* to be *uncontrived*, right?

"I did try that, Steve," Brenda says. "You'd be surprised how much egg can change flavour and texture. Too much egg is infinitely worse than too much flour. Most people would choose a dry cake rather than an excessively eggy one. Once, I was —"

And she's off again like a linguistic racehorse, running away from her pain into empty carrot cake words.

Steve spins around briefly and throws me a genuine smile. It releases some endorphins into my system, and I realise there's been a distinct lack of smiling in my life lately. It's easy to become averse to positivity when there's a lack of it in your life. You pretend to hate it, but in reality, you need it.

"Is Astrid going to be at the funeral?" I ask spontaneously.

It just came out, and nobody says anything for at least ten seconds. There's a distinctly uncomfortable vibe around the conversation.

I remember spunking on Steve's legs. I spunked on a war hero, and I deserve to feel shame for that. Astrid would laugh at that if she were here, but everyone else is quiet.

"Yes, she'll be there," Brenda says, and that's that.

I stare out the window and watch the filthy Footscray streets become grassy parks as we wind our way into the crematorium — the biggest graveyard I've ever seen.

There are rows and rows of stone memorials — some basic, with basic words, some huge with sculptures of angels and golden metal fences around them, each grave reflecting the financial status of the deceased. It's a capitalist graveyard.

Something feels peaceful about these places of death. They don't apologise for being what they are. Places that involve the living are constantly apologising for being stupid because they try to apply meaning to that which is rendered meaningless by death. Or, perhaps, death *is* the meaning. We always assume death is about meaninglessness, but is it possible that dea—*fuck it.*

The car pulls up on a gravel strip outside some church building. My first thought is that I'm glad we are indoors, as it's flaming hot outside. Next, I feel nervous as hell, not because of Keith but about the possible presence of Astrid, that enigma.

We walk up and stand with a crowd of people dressed in black outside the ancient building. Among them are dotted several people in military uniform.

I notice the smoking girl from the Zen class and smile like a marsupial at her, but she turns away in disgust. *It's justice.* I think about going over there, but I stand there, staring like a loser instead.

Everyone seems to have paired off into conversations. Lonschmoor and Brenda are doing the rounds like they are a political team or something.

Andrew is the only one not talking to anyone. He's standing next to me and staring at his phone. I don't blame him. I wish I had a phone to stare at. By now, my phone is probably sitting on a rubbish tip somewhere, its parts forever separated.

I try to think of something to say to Andrew to get his attention, but I've got nothing. My stomach is rumbling. That's something.

"My stomach's rumbling," I say to him.

He nods.

I go to say something else, but I don't know what, so it comes out as a strange sound that seems like *humf* or something.

He ignores that.

Another black car turns up. The car door opens, and just like that, Astrid is there. She's wearing an unbelievable black lace outfit, and her purple hair is now dyed jet black, which looks incredible against her pasty—I mean her *gothic* — white skin.

I'm staring at her unnaturally as she steps up to a group of people standing close by. It must be Keith's family. I'm still staring, and now I'm becoming emotional. Fuck, I'm supposed to be over this.

I wipe my eyes and turn the other way for a minute. When I look back, a man in a black suit has his hand on the small of her back. My heart rate speeds up, and a rush of hormones hits me hard.

I've felt this before but not for a long time. It's called extreme jealousy. It's the kind of thing that renders a person ugly as fuck. And that's tough because someone jealous wants to be closer to the object, but the jealousy pushes the object away. It's a torturous state. I've had a lot of time to think about it, by the way. You ignore your lover but don't want anyone else to give them attention. That's the way of modern man.

I thought it was done, yet here it is again. I can feel that compulsory scowl growing on my face. It's one of those scowls that you can't remove. It's just glued there like a cement sculpture. I didn't want this kind of fucking distraction. Today is about *Keith*, not me. Fuck.

"Who's that guy with Astrid?" I ask Andrew. He looks up from his phone for a second and squints over at Astrid, now walking, holding hands with the man.

"I'm not sure," he says. "He seems like an older man, though."

I didn't notice that myself, but Andrew has younger eyes than me. I analyse the situation and remember how Keith introduced Astrid as a nympho. Knowing what I know now, I can see he was joking. That was Keith's sense of humour. Still, she was swift to wank me off in the dining room. Maybe she is a nympho. I don't know if I could handle that. My jealousy demon wants to possess her, but I don't know if she is possessable.

A priest or one of the other types comes out of the church building and ushers everyone inside. I watch as Astrid disappears inside with her new man. He probably has money and a big cock — her man, I mean, not the priest. His cock is probably much bigger than mine, which is six inches at a push — the supposed white man's average. Still, I can ejaculate a lot. That has to count for something.

I remember the only time I had sex with Astrid. It lasted fifteen seconds or so. I think that her new man must go longer than that. He probably goes all night pumping away like Dwayne Johnson.

I'm comparing myself to him sexually, and look at the standard I've set. Why am I even jealous? My wife is dead, and who is this Astrid woman? She means nothing to me. Nothing.

Fuck. Who am I kidding? I want her, and I feel the jealous rage growing in me. I want to let go and think about Keith, but I can't. Now the anxiety is coming over the hill chanting its evil. The words are something like,

You thought you were getting better, Nicholas.
But your mind belongs to me.
If I say you bend the knee, then you bend the knee.
Always shoot for the moon?
What a fucking joke.
Why don't you take out that Longbeach
And have a good smoke?

That last bit doesn't make sense unless you know I've been saving the final Longbeach to throw into Keith's grave. It would have been a real poetic moment that you would have cried at. But now I've been forced to reveal it, it's over. To do it now would be a damn joke, and I just — fuck, these thoughts again.

I feel the hot and cold sensation washing over me. Everyone starts walking in, and I know I have to follow them, but I don't know if I can.

Andrew starts walking, then turns around to me.

"You coming?" he asks.

It's a good question. I might need a few laps around this crematorium.

"I'll be right there," I say. Then I walk in the opposite direction.

I might leave. I can probably catch a tram somewhere outside this land of death. I could go back to the house and gather some supplies. Then I could go and live on the streets. I could rent my arsehole out for money. It's not like I don't have experience. Do you need a CV for that kind of thing? Mine would say,

Six months of taking it anally using various lubricant mediums in a variety of strategic environments.

Maybe it would be easier to return to the rooftop Hi Vis restaurant and throw myself off — no Johnnie this time. Johnnie was an obstacle. That fucker is why I failed last time. This time I could throw myself off sober and —

A gravestone catches my eye, and I stop and watch for a minute. It's one of the plain stones. It says, *A.C Conrad. Loving Daughter. 1953 - 1959.*

I don't know what it means. There are probably a million Conrads in this city — or at least a few. It probably doesn't mean anything. Why should it? Why do we have to find meaning in everything? Isn't it an irritating trait of humans to do this? Why am I asking you anyway? I've lost all my damn confidence. I'm such a fucking fanny.

"Well, that's true," comes a beautiful voice behind me.

I swing around, and Astrid is standing in her black lace dress, looking unbelievable. I think about hugging her for a second, but I remember her older man and hesitate.

"It's the guy I'm seeing. His name is Chuck," she says.

I didn't fucking ask.

"What about *us*?" I say.

I regret saying that.

"What *about* us?" Astrid says, "It's not like we've had romantic nights and amazing experiences together, Nick. That's impossible while you are still so self-involved."

"I'm not self-involved anymore," I say. "I went to a Zen class with Brenda and —"

"Yeah, I heard about that, Nick, attacking women and all that."

I don't know why she's saying it like that. It's not like I did anything. I was the one that —

"Anthony isn't a woman Astrid, and *he* was the one that attacked me."

"We're different people, Nick," she says, totally ignoring what I said.

"Wrong. You're a drug addict and a psychopath," I say.

"No, Nick. I *was* a drug addict, and I'm not a psychopath. You choose to see the aspects of me that fit into your personality. I'm also a meditation practitioner. I'm a yoga teacher. I'm a woman. I'm a healer. In some ways, I'm just a young girl still. I want romance."

"I can do romance."

I can't do romance. Romance makes me want to kill.

She laughs at that.

"So, what, like flowers and shit?"

"That's not romance, Nick."

"What then?"

"You can figure it out, Mr Entrepreneur Man."

"That's not who I *am*."

Yeah, I get what she's doing.

"So, is it serious? You and Chick?"

"His name's Chuck, you idiot."

"Okay, where did you two meet?"

"It doesn't matter, Nick. Isn't today about Keith?"

Fuck, she's right. Keith is dead, and I totally forgot. It's true I'm so self-involved.

She looks down and back up, and she smiles at me. Then she holds my hand for a second.

"Are you coming?" she says.

"Yep, I'm coming."

❖

It's dark and cool in the church, which is nice. I trot up the aisle in my clicking shoes like Bing fucking Crosby, and everyone turns around and stares at me like I'm disrupting this whole memorial business or like they thought I might be bringing in Keith the corpse.

I find Brenda, and she shuffles up, making room for me where there is no room, as always. The whole row mumbles and objects as they shuffle down since they now have to make physical contact. She puts a reassuring hand on my shoulder, and I just stand there.

I look up the front and see that the box has already arrived with Keith's corpse in it. I thought they walked up the aisle with it, carrying the box on their shoulders with everyone singing,

Here comes the corpse, da da da da. Da daa da daaa etc.

They must have skipped that bit, or it's already happened, thank Christ. That part is so damn dreary.

I shake my head and hope Astrid isn't listening to me. She's up the front next to Chuck Norris, but she turns around and shoots me a brief Astrid smile. I'm okay now. She's a healer. Her smile is enough.

I *could* be more romantic, but I'm a man, so I need to learn what that means. I could Google it if I had a phone. Maybe I can borrow Brenda's phone?

Brenda reaches into her bag, and all possibilities cross my mind. Is she also psychic, and she's getting her phone out for me? Fuck, I hope she isn't psychic. Is *everyone* here a damn psychic? Am I the only dumb bastard in this church?

I expect the whole congregation to turn around and say, *Join us, Nick,* in unison, like it's some creepy horror film. But not one person does. Either they aren't all psychic, or they're ignoring me.

Brenda pulls a leaflet out of her bag and pushes it into my hands. It's one of those funeral leaflets with the order of service and the hymns, and some nice words about the deceased. There's a picture on the front of a young army officer, clean-shaven and healthy. He's strong, too, and well built — not massive like Schwarzeniver, but athletic and toned with a strong jaw.

I try to remember what Keith looked like in life, and all I can remember is how pale and skinny he was with sunken eyes and grey hair. It's not the natural transformation of age. It's the transformation of a speed addict, and it makes me sad for him. We all deal with our trauma in different ways. Keith took speed, and Lonschmoor attacked people. Me too — specifically waiters. They also had a remedy, though — the soup kitchen. It kept the trauma demon at bay. I don't have that. I'm so focused on my own shit that I can't escape it.

Astrid would like that insight. I hope she's listening.

Damn, I sound like a fucking cock — always performing like a purple clown monkey. It's not about you, you bastard. It's about Keith.

◆

We're out in a field full of holes that contain corpses again, and some guys in black and one military guy are walking up with Keith's coffin. They're going about the same teapot pace as the Zen master, and it's killing me because I need to piss now.

I could sneak off and piss behind some grave, but it's probably disrespectful to the rotting carbon atoms. Only we who are alive give a fuck about that stuff. The earth doesn't give a fuck about my piss. It's good ammonia for the soil.

I'm expecting those gunshots where everyone shits themselves, but it doesn't happen. I mean, it's not like he's one of those royals who flies a helicopter for six weeks and gets a full military state funeral. He's just your everyday, working-class war hero, or he *was* anyway.

◆

Brenda's right. The carrot cake is as dry as a camel's cock. I can see the look of shame as she wanders around, ensuring everyone's drinks are full and that everyone is stuffing homemade sausage rolls into their gobs.

I go into the kitchen and see an older lady washing endless glasses and dishes.

"I can do that," I tell her.

It's a token gesture, but I say it loud enough for people to hear and turn around to notice my selfless Samaritan act. But nobody notices. Nobody.

"Thank you," she says, drying her hands.

I want to tell her I didn't mean it, and I expected her to say *it's fine*, but it's too late.

"No problem," I say loudly as a last resort to get some attention, but nobody notices still, and now I'm fucking stuck doing the dishes.

If Akasuki were here, he might tell me to start with one cup. So I do that. I slip on the pink latex hand johnnies and I wash one cup. Then I wash another. Then I wash a plate or two. Before you can say *fuck this shit*, I've taken off my jacket, rolled up my sleeves, and I'm sweating like a bastard, scrubbing pots and that kind of crap. I don't mind if it means I don't have to socialise.

Eventually, the mass of porcelain ends, and I find myself roaming the party to find other dishes to wash — not that it's a party.

"Any dishes? Any dishes?" I say like some crockery lunatic. Still, people ignore me. Not one person to say,

Thanks for doing the dishes, Nick. You're a real legend.

No one gives a fuck anymore.

"Thanks for doing the dishes, Nick. You're a real legend." The voice is behind me. Thank Christ someone who acknowledges —

Fuck. It's Astrid. She must think I'm a right tit, but she's smiling and sipping on a glass of wine.

"Hey, you shouldn't be drinking that," I say.

"Look, I don't think you should be lecturing anyone on drinking, Mick."

She's drunk.

"Besides, I don't have a problem with alcohol, only drugs," she says.

"So you're saying alcohol isn't a drug?"

"It is. But only in the political sense. Drugs are much better than alcohol. Alcohol doesn't deserve to be a drug. It's not good enough."

We laugh and share an awkward silence.

"Don't you think it's weird that you're doing tasks and seeking acknowledgement?" she says.

"Now you mention it — yeah, it's weird."

"Nick, you should watch the people around here — see how they operate. They just get stuff done. Nobody asks to be noticed. The reward is the job getting done."

Now I feel like a real knobend.

"Don't feel like that, Nick. It's just part of growing up, getting over your ego."

I'm not mad. I'm not feeling anything. I'm just so stoked that she's speaking to me. Fuck me. I'm in love with her.

She puts her head down and blushes a bit.

"I'm sorry," I say. "Fuck, I don't know how to be around you with these thoughts."

"You're gonna be alright, Nick," she says as if I'm never going to see her again.

Chuck comes up and interrupts our moment.

"Are you ready?" he says, touching her back.

My head is shaking involuntarily.

"Chuck, this is Nick. Nick, this is Chuck," she says, staring at me the whole time.

I shake Chuck's manly hand with my pink rubber hand, but I stare at *her* the entire time. I want to say something witty about Chuck, but I don't. Because. Well. Because I love her. Also, it's the damn method.

She leaves me with an aching burning in my stomach. It's a feeling that she's going away or that Chuck will buy her some fucking big diamond ring and propose, and she'll say yes, and before you know it, she's got kids.

I need to get back to the dishes.

I discover the box-shaped item in my right pocket, which, it turns out, is the last Longbeach. I remember that I was going to lob it in Keith's grave when they buried him, but I either forgot or didn't bother because I spoiled the moment in advance. Those things have to be spontaneous, or it's just pathetic. Come to think of it, *everything* has to be spontaneous, or it's just pathetic.

Most of the people are leaving. It's not just Astrid and Chuck. Or is it Chuck and Astrid? Chastrid? Asstuck?

Chuck — what a dumb fucking name. He's not even American. What does it mean, anyway? Did his mother like chuck steak? Or does it mean to chuck something like a throwing star or a knife or something?

Some bald guy has taken over the dishes, that opportunistic bastard. He didn't even ask me if it was okay. Can't he see I'm still wearing these damn rubber gloves? Or does he think it's some deranged fashion choice?

The woman I took over from thanks him for doing it like he's responsible for the whole pile. This prick has washed two dishes and is taking all the credit. For a second, I want to stab him in the neck with a spoon handle, but I remember what Astrid said about things getting done being its own reward, so I head outside instead.

I hold the last Longbeach up to the sky and nod at imaginary Keith sitting on a cloud with — well fuck knows — Eddie Van Halen, John

Wayne, JFK — whoever his damn heroes are. Regardless, he's been restored to his young soldier self and —

"What are you *doing*?" comes a high-pitched voice behind me.

It's a young child — a boy if I observe correctly. And he's staring at me like I'm a mad bastard. Kids have a way of making you feel like an absolute twat.

"Nothing," I say. "Where are your parents?"

The kid points inside and then looks down, making me feel sorry for the little shit. But what am I meant to say? It's complicated.

Listen, Kid. I'm toasting Keith with a cheap Longbeach, okay?

The kid wouldn't get it. He doesn't know what this Longbeach means. But maybe he's right. Maybe I *am* a mad bastard.

He goes to walk off.

"Hey, Kid," I say.

He looks back, hopefully. It feels strangely like the moment in the cafe with Keith. I have to say something meaningful. I have to make this moment poetic.

"Do you have a light?" I say.

Brenda appears and saves the situation. She pats the kid on the head, pulls out a cheap plastic lighter and lights up the last Longbeach for me.

Zero

I should be dead by this point, and I'm not. And I just don't know whether I'm grateful for that. I *think* I am. I know I would be a lot more if Chuck would fuck off.

I realise this is all Keith's fault. If it weren't for that skinny-arsed fucker I would have leapt off that building like Neo. Or would I? Either the whole thing was his fault, or he saved my life by dying.

Brenda pulls out an envelope from her pocket and hands it to me.

"What's this?" I ask.

I open the envelope, and there is a wad of hundred-dollar notes. Brenda smiles.

"It's from Keith," she says. "He had a hidden stash of cash that he wanted to be distributed, and your name was the last person on his list."

"But, the soup kitchen?" I say. "The retreat — he didn't even need the money?"

She tilts her head as if to tell me she doesn't know or doesn't care, or both.

"Keith just wanted to be involved with everyone doing things, Nick," she says. "He liked to organise events. The Save The Soup Kitchen Plan was his way of bringing everyone together in a project."

That weasel fuck.

I count the money. It's about three grand.

"It's about three grand," I say.

She nods and starts heading inside.

"Brenda," I say.

"Yes, love."

"Is there anything I can do to help with the soup kitchen, retreat, or anything?" It seems I'm only saying it because of the money, but I'm not — I don't think.

She smiles again and takes the little boy's hand.

"Come on, Keith," she says.

"What? The kid's name is Keith?"

"Yes, Nick. This is Keith. He's Keith's grandson—"

Someone just dropped a fucking piano on my head.

"You've already done a lot, Nick, and let's not forget the whole thing was your idea,"

"It was?" I say.

"Yes," she says. "Anyway, it'll be nice if you can join us at the retreat. There'll be plenty to help out with." She smiles once more and ushers Keith Junior inside.

And now I'm left standing out here in the stinking sun with the fucking crickets, crying like a damn pink baby, and not knowing if it's because of the invitation to the retreat or the shock of Keith having a family or the realisation that I never even spoke to any of them at the funeral — or the post-corpus cash, or the fact that I'm terrified that I'll never see Astrid again or the urge to chase after her and stop her at the airport like it's some Hollywood movie even though she isn't even going to the airport, or the fact that I should have just chucked the Longbeach in the grave instead of smoking the damn thing.

Or.

Because.

For the first time in a very, very long time,

I think I'm gonna be alright.

The Road

It's the day of the retreat, and I'm anxious as fuck.

It's not just because I'll see Astrid today or because Big Cock Chuck might be at the retreat. It's also because the last time I tried to meditate, it didn't go well, and I ended up in a headlock, and the whole thing led to me being on top of a building at 2 am.

And I know it's more complicated than that.

I'm in the shower, scrubbing myself with someone else's loofah and someone else's shower gel. The gel is a cheap bastard brand of carcinogenic blue shit from some shitty supermarket, so I don't feel bad about using it.

I feel mildly guilty about using the loofah, though. Would I want to scrub my cock with a loofah that had been chuffed up someone's arsehole scrubbing out the dried shit particles from last night's curry? I wouldn't.

So I put the loofah back and have one of those unsatisfying non-scrub bare-hand showers where you hardly feel clean at the end. I have to now. It's the damn method.

I consider having a shower wank but decline for two reasons. First, I've never been good at the standing wank. That kind of thing takes practice, and people like me need gravity to get the blood to where it needs to go. Secondly, it's the day of the retreat, and while I'm pumped about seeing Astrid, I can't stop thinking about Chuck with his big dick inside her. And sure, part of me is turned on by that, but mostly I'm jealous as fuck. So I get out and towel myself dry instead. I brush my teef with an expensive toofbrush and expensive toofpaste I bought from the shop yesterday when I forgot I might need a loofah and some expensive shower gel.

Now I'm slipping on a soft, brand-new cotton shirt. I'm like Richard fucking Branson these days, thanks to Keith. You'd think I was wearing gold cufflinks and driving a damn Bentley the way I'm acting.

I wander back into Astrid's room and pull out the giant Kmart bag I left on the end of her bed. I take out a box that contains a brand-new Thermomix. Then I negotiate all of the formaldehyde-soaked wrappings, take the worked steel appliance to the kitchen and slot it into where the old one was.

It's the kind of moment I should shed a tear at, but I don't because I see through the vanity of it all. Corpses don't need new kitchen appliances. I bought this for myself to ease the guilt. It's a purely selfish decision.

For a second, I consider taking it back because I realise I've ruined the poetic moment yet again. It's not spontaneous anymore. It's simply pathetic. But, I hear the unmistakable squeaky rear diff as Keith's shit cream Falcon pulls up out front, and the lame toot takes me back to that first day at Footscray station when Keith picked me up, and for a second, I get a bit choked up.

Fuck it.

I slip on my new environmentally friendly bamboo shoes, which I bought two days ago, while feeling the urge to become an out-and-out hippy to impress Astrid.

I grab the thirty-dollar gourmet vegetarian quiche from the fridge I bought as an 'offering' for the Zen retreat, and I head out the door.

"Morning, Nicholas," says Sergeant Lonschmoor from the driver's seat. He is no longer in uniform, but I still feel the tremendous urge to stand up straight and salute him, and before I can purge the fantasy, it happens.

"Good morning, Sergeant," I say, feeling like an absolute twat who has lost control of his body.

I shake my head, crouching into the passenger seat.

"Sorry about that," I say, preparing to launch into an in-depth rant about how I'm barely in control of my body and mind. But I don't get that far.

"Nobody salutes sergeants, Nicholas. We are non-commissioned officers," says Steve Lonschmoor, the civilian. "But thanks, anyway, Mate."

He pulls away from the halfway house and takes off up the road at twenty kilometres per hour like the pensioner he is.

"How are you feeling today anyway?" he asks.

I wind down the window. The air's a little cooler, and it could rain later. That's the summary of the internal and external weather, but I only think it, and the moment passes. It's not spontaneous anymore, so I let it slide back into the ether.

"Not bad, Steve," I say instead. It's a shit line. It lacks respect for the war hero. It says that I only have the generic line for you. You aren't worthy of my brain power Steve, despite your medals and heroics.

"Bit nervous about the retreat," I say. That's more like it.

It's not that I'm nervous about the actual retreat. As long as there are chairs, it'll be fine. I'm more worried about — well, I'm not going into it again. You've heard that shit already, and I —

Steve Lonschmoor nods and clears his throat.

"Are you nervous about the meditation or that a certain lady will be there?" he says.

He's all over this. When he asked about my feelings, he meant it. It's a skill I need to develop, asking a question and then actually listening to and processing the answer.

"Yeah, it's mostly Astrid," I tell him. My stomach does a flip when I say her name.

"Do you think things between her and Chunk are serious?" I ask like he is Doctor Phil or something.

He smiles in a way that symbolises laughter because I called Chuck, Chunk. I mean, sure, he probably won't get a complete Goonies reference if I take it further, but still, I appreciate the Lonschmoor smile. It's a rare creature, indeed.

We pull up at some traffic lights, and I take a scout around while Doctor Phil prepares his answer to my question. There's a pickup truck carrying a van, and it looks like they are fucking in the way insects fuck, or dogs, for that matter — one on the back humping away, and I wonder if insects or dogs know how to give head. We've all seen them *licking* cock — dogs, that is, not insects —but do they know how to suck? — I mean, how to really suck? — how to give head like Gary Busey? — how to massage the balls in a mildly aggressive way while sucking shaft like an industrial humanoid hooker?

It's a disturbing train of thought which nearly launches a full-scale panic attack.

"Astrid's pregnant, Nicholas," Lonschmoor says suddenly and quite loudly.

I feel my insides turn to green and red flames. My whole body burns like I have been plunged into the depths of some hell. The sky turns black, and all the demons fly out from a grid underneath the insect trucks. The panic turns to rage.

I want to schlock Chuck in the throat with a silver spoon handle. I want to — fuck it. I don't know. I want to drink. Why am I going to this retreat anyway? Who are these damn people? I don't know any of them.

"So, what? That's fucking it then, is it?" I say.

We've pulled off again, and we're heading through an industrial estate.

"I'm not sure what you mean, Nicholas," he says. "Did you hear what I said?"

"Yeah, you said Astrid is pregnant, which means Big Dick Chunk has chucked his spunk in her, and now they are going to live happily ever after in his mansion in Connecticut with his three dogs, and she's gonna make his ravioli every night when he comes home from work and — *fuck.*"

"It's *yours*, Nicholas," Lonschmoor says, interrupting my insane tirade.

A rapid-fire heartbeat and a cold sensation replace the burning in my body. For a few seconds, everything stops. The earth stops spinning, I can feel the blood in my veins and the atoms in my heart, and I can count the exact number of protons in the universe.

"It's mine?" I need clarification. I couldn't bear it if I misunderstood what he just told me. "Like — the baby — is mine?"

"Yes."

"*Hmmm,*" I say like some tight-sphincter professor analysing a physics problem. It's not PCP-level physics, though. It's A-level biology. I put my junk in her trunk, and I spunked, and now she's schmunked, and it's got fuck all to do with Chunk.

For some reason, I get an erection, and it's not the usual three-quarter style rock-on either. It's full, and that's something I haven't experienced in, well —

"*Hmmm,*" I say again.

I know I should be terrified of becoming a father, especially given the antics of the last few weeks, but I'm not. I'm not even considering the baby. I'm just trying to assimilate the intense bliss which is filling my body, beginning in this tiny blue light in my perineum and spreading out to all regions of this living corpus mortuum known only as Nicholas Conrad.

"Can you pull over for a minute?" I say to Steve, and he swings the shit cream Falcon into a loading zone between two shabby white vans and flicks off the engine. He winds down his window and stares into the grey wind and the crowds of bogan citizens going about their bogan business.

"Sorry, Nicholas," he says. "I shouldn't have sprung it on you like that."

I can't be mad at him because I do the same myself. I also can't imagine what the alternative would be. Should he have revealed this to me one word every ten seconds, or even one letter, by horseback messenger every three months? That would have been far too time-consuming. My child would be in their twenties by the time I learned of their existence.

The straight news was undoubtedly the only choice.

I want to share this with Steve, but I can't. I'm too busy wondering what happens next in all of this.

I think about Astrid and wonder if she is aware that Steve just told me. I hope she isn't and that she's too busy setting up the retreat and —

"Are you okay, Nicholas?" Steve asks.

If okay is a city, then I'm the capital city. If okay is a sport, I'm the world champion. If okay is a chocolate bar, then I'm a fat bastard. No, that last one doesn't work. I'll go number one.

"If I'm a city, then okay is—" No, that's not it.

I nod and say,

"Yes."

No fancy words are needed.

"Are you sure about all this?" I ask.

"Yep, I'm sure, Mate."

"So, when did she tell you, and how do you know it's mine?"

I feel bad dumping my questions on a war hero, but I need answers. I need to be sure. I couldn't bear it if he had made a mistake and she wasn't pregnant or, even worse if the baby was Chuck's.

"I'm sure Nicholas — about *all* of it. Astrid called me a couple of days ago to wish me goodbye, and that's when she told me. She said not to tell you though because she wanted to tell you herself and —"

He starts up the car engine.

"And *what*, Steve?"

"*Nothing.*"

"Steve, *please?*"

He gives me the Lonschmoor smile again and starts driving again.

"She said she wasn't sure if you were ready to be involved."

My stomach does one of those flips again.

"Of course I'm ready," I say aggressively.

A mother walking her baby past the car turns and scowls at me. And damn, I hope that isn't one of those signs. I mean, what the fuck could she mean by that anyway?

"What do you think she means by that anyway?" I ask Steve.

He pulls the car out into traffic and takes a deep breath.

"Not sure," he says. "She could mean that she thinks you might not *want* to be involved or might not be ready—as in — *emotionally.*"

"What the fuck?" I say, shaking my head at the road ahead. Then I think about what she's seen of me in the last few weeks, and I come to my senses. Why *wouldn't* she believe that? I mean, I'm doing it again. I'm doing what she said I do — not seeing because I'm lost in my own shit.

Of course, I want her to think I'm ready, but all she sees is a lunatic. And, let's face it, this is a *real-life* baby we're talking about here. A real-life — wow. My face cramps, and the tears flow again.

Fuck.

The sergeant puts his hand on my thigh like he is trying to court me, and I just hope he keeps his hand closer to my knee as my erection is still at full salute.

He pats my thigh once and takes his hand away. We both know it was a weird move, but he was driving and wanted to comfort me, so it was the only option, and I'm grateful for that.

I don't know if there's much more to say. I have to speak to Astrid, and I guess I'm going to see her in twenty minutes or so. I wipe my eyes on my Richard Branson shirt, and I realise that Astrid was calling to say goodbye to Lonschmoor.

"Why was Astrid saying goodbye?" I ask.

Now Lonschmoor is nodding.

"I'm hitting the road, Nicholas."

"What? After the retreat?"

"No, I'm not going to the retreat. Well, not to your retreat anyway. There's a retreat up North where they take Ayahuasca. It's meant to be good for healing the past. Keith and I talked about it for years, and we were meant to do it together. And if I'm honest, I only stuck around to help Keith with the soup kitchen. Now that he is gone, I figured I would do it to honour Keith's memory."

Tears are streaming down my face now.

I tried to hit those poetic moments — the cigarette in the grave, the Thermomix —but I fucked them. This is another one of those moments. Sergeant Steve Lonschmoor knows how to do it. It's a Thelma and Louise moment, and I want him to drive the shit cream Falcon off a cliff with both of us in it.

I've heard a bit about Ayahuasca. It's a potent drug that takes you back into the womb or some shit. And for a second, I want to go to the retreat with him, but then I remember Astrid is pregnant with my baby.

We drive for the next ten minutes in almost total silence, and I wonder how I managed to get Astrid pregnant with around twenty seconds of penetration. Potent sperm — that's what it is. It's probably my best quality. I should add it to my CV.

A potent, voluminous spunker with many hours of experience in schlepping out gallons of white stuff in a variety of strategic environments.

"Steve, do you have children?" I ask.

"Never happened for me, Mate," he says. "I got my dick blown off during the war, so I've never been able to conceive."

I look at his pale face for signs of humour, but I don't see a scratch. His face is stone cold, focused on the road ahead.

Fuck. It's no wonder he lost it when I spunked on his legs. Imagine having no cock. Imagine being horny as fuck but not being able to have a wank. If it were me, I'd have to fuck myself up the arse with something. I'd probably have a whole collection of dildos of various colours and sizes, from the tiny silver slim Jim to the giant purple ring stretcher.

He gives me a smile that tells me either he's made his peace with being shaftless or he's taking the piss.

"I took Keith's Thermomix," I say spontaneously.

If I examine the logic, some part of my brain was trying to make up for the fact that Lonschmoor had his cock blown off by confessing my theft. He has no cock, whereas I'm a filthy robber. It makes perfect sense when you think about it.

"What do you mean?" Lonschmoor says. He has a slightly less friendly look on his face, and I remember that he can eat my neck out like a fucking wolf and that I have turned him into this calm war hero father figure in my mind, and it's just not like that at all.

"I'd like to retract that last statement," I say like it's an episode of Law and Order or whatever. But I realise it's sitting in my chest, and I have to confess fully, even if it means getting my throat eaten out.

I'm past resistance anyway. Let it be.

"Okay, I stole Keith's Thermomix and sold it for cash to buy alcohol the night you found me. I think it was that night, anyway. I can't really remember. It was such a blur."

"I wondered what happened to that," he says with a smirk. "I vaguely remember you saying something about a Thermomix when we were on the roof."

He drives, and nothing more is said.

It's pretty easy this confession business—no wonder the Christians love it. You just say what you did, and that's the end. Maybe you say a few Hail Mandys or whatever, and you're saved from hell—Christian hell, that is.

Surely you don't want to end up in Christian heaven either — an eternity with your relatives? No thanks.

Akasuki used to say Christian heaven is like Buddhist hell. He said Buddhists practice to avoid both heaven *and* hell.

Anyway, where was I, Father Lonschmoor? What else can I confess?

"I got fucked in prison," I say.

I could have taken it slower. Maybe I could have confessed my whiskey robbery. No silver slim Jims here. Straight to the purple ring stretcher.

Confession is supposed to be about bad things you've done, not things that have happened *to* you. And yet, getting fucked by Arsehole Taylor has that energy of me having done something wrong.

I'm waiting for his response, but he says nothing, and I consider repeating it as in — *Steve. Are you deaf?*

Fuck it. He heard it anyway, and now we are sitting in awkward silence. I realise that I went from, *I stole a kitchen appliance* to *I got fucked in prison* in a matter of seconds, and Steve Lonschmoor is not my therapist, he is a war hero, and so he *should* remain silent for long enough for me to change the damn subject.

"So, do you like Boney M?" I say. It's in the top ten most random things I have said this week. If he says yes, I'll have to keep going and explain why I asked, which is a problem since I don't know any songs by Boney M.

"I'm sorry to hear that, Nicholas," he says.

"Thanks," I say. I don't know what I expected — maybe some counselling session. I don't even know why I said it, and I regret it.

It was a confession, and maybe at some sick level, I'm trying to bond with him by showing that I, too, have some form of PTSD. Maybe I wanted some kind of session where I talk, and he gives me fatherly advice about life and all that. But then I remember it's confession. You tell it, and it's gone.

Hail Mandy, full of grass etc.

We pull up at this large gate, and Lonschmoor winds his window down at the intercom. There's a deranged buzz, and a voice says something like

Crabs.

Then Steve says,

Stevie Nicks — or something like that, and the gate opens.

It's secret Zen code.

We take off through the gate into this luxurious paradise of grass and plants with a few random peacocks scattered around.

My hands are shaking, and I'm sweating like Justin Beaver in a sauna as we roll up towards a beautiful white temple with a gold roof.

I'm shitting myself because I know I'm about to see her. Yet there's still some judgemental narrative in my head that curses these Zen people for claiming to be non-religious and non-material and yet performing all these bizarre rituals and putting gold roofs on temples.

Steve parks the car among a few others and turns off the engine.

My head is spinning.

"Can I come with you to the drug retreat?" I say. "I mean, can we just go now? Please?"

He puts his hand on my shoulder this time.

"Breathe deeply," he says.

I look into his eyes as I breathe, and I feel alright. How could I have judged this war hero as a crooked vampire? Perception is — well, perception is —

"Perception is nine-tenths of the law," I say. I'm not sure exactly what it means, but Steve nods his agreement.

"Are you alright, Son?" he says. It's Keith's language. He's channelling Keith now, and it makes me feel alright.

"I think so," I say.

We climb out into the murky air, and I grab my massacred vegetarian quiche.

"Don't offer that," Steve says, opening the boot. "Take these instead."

He hands me a bunch of beautiful white flowers, and I feel the tears again.

"Don't *you* want to offer these?" I ask.

"No, Mate. I'm not coming in. I'm gonna shoot off."

Fuck.

We stand there for a second, looking at each other and listening to the wind.

"Any last advice?" I say, taking one last glimpse at the man who saved my life, who inspired me to become better, to do better, the man who —

Fuck. Stop being a *fanny.*

He grabs my hand and shakes it.

"Always shoot for the moon, Kid," he says. Then he lets go of my hand and stands to attention, and I do the same, remembering not to salute.

Sergeant Steve Lonschmoor walks around and gets back into Keith's shit-cream Falcon. I lean in via the open passenger window as he starts the car.

"What does that mean?" I ask. "What does always shoot for the moon mean?"

He puts on his aviator sunglasses like he is Tom Cruise.

"No idea, Mate," he says. "Astrid said it to me the last time we spoke. I'd say it probably means *don't waste your life*, Nicholas,"

We nod at each other one more time, and the shit cream Falcon takes off back down the driveway, leaving a cloud of dry white dust forming around me.

I wait for the dust to settle. Then, I turn around and face the golden building — Branson shirt on, flowers in hand.

"Don't waste your life, Nicholas," I whisper to myself.

I take three deep breaths and put one foot in front of the other.

Refuge

Everyone's staring at me when I walk in.

There's a mixture of strange looks, scowls and laughter, and I realise that Anthony Weasley must have told my story to everyone — about him putting me in a headlock. I'm fine with it. I'm only here for Astrid, I think. Well, I'm sort of here to meditate as well — just mainly for —

I'm about to take a seat on a brown plastic chair at the back, and I notice myself in the mirror. I'm white. I'm *really* white. I'm covered head to toe in white dust. It's the final bite of Count Lunchmore, that vampire bastard. He sunk his greasy brown teeth into my ego for the last time, and now I'm surrounded by people laughing.

I'm not laughing with them per se, but there's no chance of shedding a tear either. I'm too busy looking around for the mother of my future child. She isn't anywhere, but there's a big empty seat up the front surrounded by flowers and a big water jug on the table. That's it. We're still in the *waiting* stage. At some point, she'll walk out toward the throne at an excruciatingly ball-shrinking pace. Then she'll clear her throat and —

Most of the congregation have turned back to the front now, and sure, I should go and wash my face, but I know she is due at any moment, and I'm just not going to miss that for a clean look. So, I sit instead and stare at the door like a dog waiting for its —

I feel the sudden cold of a cloth on my face, and the stink of antiseptic something, and Brenda is standing in front of me, wiping my face. For a second, the smell reminds me of whiskey and that night, and I get a flash of depression, but it's just not going to last. Nothing can stop this waterfall of positivity that's washing over me in a dangerously extreme way.

I look up at Brenda's face again.

"I'm sorry, Brenda," I say.

I'm unsure if that's the fifth or the seventh time I have apologised to her this week, but it doesn't matter.

"It's okay, love," she says, smiling back at me and squeezing my cheeks like my primary school teacher, Miss Sampson, reincarnated. She takes my white flowers and wanders back around to the front. I watch her as she places the flowers in a vase on the shrine, then effortlessly crouches back down into that impossible cross-legged position.

The woman next to her swings around and blasts me with a big smile and a wave. It's Berthandra, that sweet woman. I send her back a genuine smile that gives me a rush of energy from my brain.

I wave in an over-the-top way, like I'm Tom Hanks waving from a train, and for a second, I feel embarrassed, but she laughs and smiles even more, and I feel like our joy is going to spill over into some song-and-dance like this is a Zen musical or something.

I'm about to jump up and break into my big tap scene when the person next to Berthandra turns around, and I feel all the blood leave my face, and the serotonin centres all slam their doors and put a sign out that says, *closed for winter.* It's Anthony Weasley, the prick who assaulted me at the last meditation.

For a few seconds, I panic, but then I want to laugh and tell him what he did was hilarious, and it ended up helping, so I shoot him a smile and wave. He responds with a scowl and a middle finger.

Justice.

The white double doors open, and everyone goes quiet and bends over slightly. A young Dean Cain-looking character in fisherman's pants with a porno moustache comes strolling out. He opens the door and shuffles things around on the main table. This is his way of letting people know he's important — that Dean Cain means something in this place.

Humans love letting people know they *mean* something, and I'd like to say that no one gives a fuck, but in this case, they do. They *all* want to be Dean Cain shuffling papers around for the teacher and having the whole room desire to be just as important.

That fucking prick. I hope he hasn't been trying to get into bed with Astrid. That's what happens. The lure of these spiritual teachers and —

Fuck. I'm being a jealous bastard again. It's not the method. Besides, we are having a baby together. There's nothing that can stand in our way now unless I have a heart attack because my heart is nearly popping out of my chest, like in that scene in Alien or whatever.

I've been so busy wondering about Dean Cain that I didn't notice Astrid has walked into the room and is crouched down talking to Brenda in the front row. No ceremony, no pomp, no ball-shrinking slow walks. She's just being *normal.*

She's wearing a black robe with her hair tied above her head in a bun, and I wonder if she heard my jealous rant about Dean Cain, but I doubt it. She looks different here — focused and intense, and her hair is *naturally* light brown.

She walks back to the throne, sits cross-legged, and everyone does the De La Soul bow. I know how to do it now, so I bow three times and realise I'm bowing to *her*, and I'm okay with it. It feels more natural than bowing to some old Asian gentleman. But for some reason, I feel like I'm also bowing to Akasuki, and for a second, I get a lump in my throat and feel a few drops of spontaneous gratitude for that Zen bastard, and I hope he's doing alright.

Everyone sits down, and there's silence for a few moments before Astrid chants something, and a bunch of the people up the front join in.

I do my usual subconscious racist analysis of the room and see mostly Western people with a couple of Indians and Asians dotted around. And yet we are chanting in a foreign language again. It sounds like Japanese, which is much gruntier and less whiny than Chinese.

I look along to my right. I notice the fat man who sat next to me at Brenda's Zen show, and I give him a nod. He smiles back while chanting.

I look to the left. There are two empty seats and then a short man who looks like Eddie the Eagle, that shit ski jumper from the eighties. He looks at me, and I give him a nod. He ignores me and continues chanting.

Now Dean Cain arrives at our row and begins distributing papers to everyone. He gets to me, smiles, and hands me the sheet. I give him the nod and attempt to smile, but it comes out as a scowl.

"I'm sorry," I say, realising immediately it doesn't make sense.

There's a knack to these things — being part of a social group. You need to have at least partial control over your body and mind. I don't think I'm there yet. I'm still controlled by the thoughts and emotions that come into my head. I mean, that's obvious. I don't need to explain that to you.

I look down at the paper and read the first section.

The Threefold Refuge Prayer:

From now until I reach enlightenment
I take refuge in the three jewels
To free all sentient beings from samsara
I generate Bodhicitta as aspiration, as action,
and in its absolute meaning. (x 3)

I remember this refuge thing from last time, even though I have no idea what it means. Below are some Japanese characters and some phonetics. I finally match the chanting to the phonetics and open my mouth to join in, but the chanting stops instantly.

For a second, I get pissed off at Dean Cain for giving me the sheet when the chanting had almost finished. He might be important, but he's still a useless prick. And he better not be trying to sleep with Astrid. I'll knee him in the teeth. I'll leap up like Ken Masters and flying kick the little Superman bastard. I'll wear kryptonite boots when I do it too. That fucker will bleed all over the —

Fuck

Deep breath

Astrid clears her throat, but not in a disgusting way. It's the sexiest throat-clearing I've ever heard.

"First of all, I just want to thank everyone for making it here in one piece," she says. "Since this is samsara, the causes of death are far more common than the causes of life, so congratulations on getting this far."

Everyone laughs.

Was that a joke? I'm not sure what's funny about that. I mean, she's right, and that's downright scary. Or I suppose it is now I care about living. It exposes *me* as a useless prick too. I dedicated a whole night to killing myself and couldn't pull it off.

"I suppose that means we all have some kind of decent karma," she says.

Some people are still laughing. It's not a fucking comedy show, for fuck's sake. *Shut up and have some respect.*

I nearly say that out loud and realise people like me, who have little control over their body and mind, should avoid thinking as much as possible at these times.

I take three deep breaths as Astrid seems to do the same, closing her eyes. Then she opens them and glances at me for a brief second, almost causing my perineum to explode with joy.

"In the traditional Buddha's teachings, we often hear about celestial and supernatural beings attending as well as humans and animals," she says. "And I notice we have at least one ghost with us today, so thank you for leaving your ghostly realm and being with us,"

There's more laughter. This time, it's much more manic, like she just told the joke of the year.

For a second, I think I'm not cut out for this bizarre Zen humour until at least fifty per cent of the crowd turn around and look at me while laughing, and I look back at Astrid, who is looking at me with a beautiful grin.

It's *me*. I'm the ghost with my dusty white exterior. I'm Casper the Friendly Cock. I get it. It's hilarious, but she needs to move on.

There's silence now except for one filthy motherfucker in the third row who is blowing their nose.

"The aim of meditation," Astrid says, "is to control the mind."

She nods as if listening to an ancient podcast. "The basic methods of Zen fall under three categories: Discipline, Concentration and wisdom. The *discipline* aspect is designed to create a stable ground of physical and moral peace within which the practice of concentration or samatha can bear fruit. Then, the practice of *concentration* creates a stable ground of mental peace within which the practice of *wisdom* or vipassana can bear fruit. From there, the procedure is to continuously integrate and re-ignite one's practice of insight until it becomes an unbroken experience. The retreat we are about to undergo is concerned mainly with the practice of concentration or meditation. So during the retreat, we will practise the five ethical trainings that comprise the basic level of *discipline*. They are as follows: First, we will refrain from *killing*. That means during this retreat, you should avoid killing or causing physical harm to any living being, from the tiniest insect up to the person coughing in the row in front."

There's laughter again, and I think it's general laughter, but I'm convinced it's directed at me. I don't see any sign of the smoking girl. I have to say it's a good rule. I'm feeling much better, but after my last meditation attempt, I can't guarantee that I won't attempt to stab Weasley or Dean Cain with a blunt spoon. But it's not an option now. Astrid says no killing, so that's just how it has to be.

"Secondly, we will refrain from *false speech*. In other words, we must speak the truth at all times."

I'm a bit more disturbed by this second one. Surely there are times when lying is appropriate. Surely, I have to lie to Anthony Weasley when I tell him I accept that he is a bloke. Isn't that the *method*? Or does no lying mean I have to tell him that because he has tits and a vagina, he is a damn woman in my book? It's ambiguous at best.

Will I have to tell Berthandra what amazing tits she has? Surely it's best to pretend I don't see them. Surely it's —

Astrid has stopped talking now, and she's looking right at me. And it's not with her perfect smile. It's that ball-shattering look that says, *this is the kind of talk that broke the porcelain horse*. In fact, that's exactly what she's communicating to me.

I know. I have to remember the method. Okay, okay, no lies. Check. *Next*.

"Thirdly," she says, looking down at her sheet again. "We will refrain from *stealing* from others."

I have no problem with that one. It's not like there are bottles of Johnnie or Thermomixes to be had here. The only thing to be stolen here is people's affection.

"Fourthly, we will refrain from *intoxicants*. Of course, if you are on medication, please see John. And, of course, tea and coffee will be served during breaks, so don't panic."

More giggles, and I wonder if smoking is allowed. It's probably not, which is probably why the smoking girl isn't here.

"Finally, we will refrain from *sexual misconduct*."

Sexual misconduct. That's an interesting one. I thought that one was compulsory in religious circles. And what does *misconduct* mean anyway? Does it mean to refrain from flashing my cock to other participants during meditation sessions or —

"In our case." Astrid interrupts my train of thought. "It means refraining from *all* sexual activity, whether with others or with oneself."

What? Is she serious? I mean, I didn't intend to sleep with Astrid again this weekend, but at least I was planning to do it in my head while having a good wank. That's just not fair. And I'd usually do it anyway. I've never been one for rules, but she knows *everything*. She would know.

Astrid's smiling now, and she isn't looking at me, but I know it's intended for me, and it gives me a hard-on. Is this sexual misconduct?

"With all that in mind," she says, "let's close our eyes and get acquainted with the breath."

Everyone shuffles and straightens their backs, and I do the same while pretending to know what I'm doing.

I'm okay with all of this. *The aim of meditation is to control the mind.* And if there's one thing I need to do more than anything, it's control this damn mind. And sure, if I examined my motivation, I might find that I want to meditate to impress Astrid and prove myself to be a worthy lover and father, which, let's face it, is a little psychotic. And I'm sure there are things to be said in Zen about motivation. But I don't know if I can muster any other kind of motivation. And if it works — I mean, if this meditation thing works, who would care what the reason for it was? *Surely I'm right?*

I open my eyes, and there she is. Everyone has their eyes closed except us. She is luminous, looking at me like no one can see us. She smiles and then closes her eyes again.

I'm enlightened. There is nothing more real than this.
When I hear her voice, I'm listening to the Buddha.
Maybe you don't need to be Asian.

Maybe you don't even need a cock.
You probably do need good legs, though.

And we breathe. All of us together breathe.
All of the freaks and geeks.
The men and women and the others breathe
Because that's what we have in common.
We all need oxygen.
It's our lowest common denominator.

◆

Afterwards, I'm sitting outside on a small stone wall, staring at a yellow flower that seems so beautiful that it makes me want to cry. Has someone slipped me a mickey, or has the meditation already had some effect?

"You've been through a lot, Nick."

I look up, and it's Astrid in her black robe with her light brown hair, no makeup, and a faceful of freckles that make me want to melt into her.

I stand up and start to move in for the hug but immediately back off and press my palms together as if praying, and I say,

"Konichiwa," instead.

"I'm sorry," I say. "It just came out,"

She smiles, goes a little red, looks down like a young girl, and then looks back at me.

"What I mean, Nick, is you've been through a lot, and your reaction to the flower is just your body and mind feeling a little relief. It's important not to make a big deal of the bliss. It's just an amplified lack of pain. It's like if you had spent weeks burning in hell, living in Footscray would seem like heaven."

We both laugh.

"I feel like I've been burning in hell for weeks," I say.

There's a miniature silence — no crickets here, only gentle birds.

"Steve Lonschmoor said —" I say, but I don't know how to word the rest. "How's Chuck?" I say instead.

"I'm *pregnant*, Nick," she says.

I draw another deep breath.

"I know," I say. What is to be said next, though? I need to listen to a podcast or something.

"So, what does that mean for *us*?" I hate myself for saying the words. I wanted it to be a poetic moment, but I'm stuffing it up yet again.

Fuck these poetic moments.

"I meant to say —"

This is it, Conrad. This is your big moment. Don't screw it up. Say the right thing.

"— will you be my *girlfriend*?"

It's basically what a twelve-year-old says to another twelve-year-old, and maybe that's the key. Aren't we all just children pretending we are adults? Is that what this fucking tension in my balls is? Is it just the pressure to be an adult?

Astrid giggles.

"You know, I wasn't sure you were ready for a child Nick," she says. "I'm still not sure. So, you'll understand if I'm a bit hesitant to —"

She looks down and then looks at me again. She takes a step closer and takes hold of my hand.

Fuck. Is she still with Chuck? Maybe Chuck is being reasonable about it. Maybe he's excited about being a stepfather. Maybe he shoots blanks, and this is his one good opportunity. Maybe he is —

"Nick, of course, I broke up with Chuck as soon as I found out," she says. "Let's take it slowly, though. First, you agree to meditate every day and not drink."

I nod. That's easy. I'd throw myself off a building if she asked me to.

"Second, you need to get better at the sex."

I feel the flames go to my face.

"Astrid, I usually am better — much better," I say, looking at her desperately and then watching as she breaks into laughter again.

She leans in and puts her lips next to my ear.

"Thirdly," she whispers, "buy your own underwear, Nick."

I feel the blood rush to my face, and it's fine. She's smiling. She's utterly beautiful.

I feel a nudge against my right knee, and a golden retriever is sitting and looking up at me, panting. I let go of Astrid's hand and squat down slowly, stroking its head and putting my face toward its face. It licks me on the nose.

"Who are you?" I say. "Where did you come from?"

"This is *Yeshe*," Astrid says. "She's mine."

I remember the golden puppy in Astrid's photo, and I'm about to ask if that was Yeshe, but I stop myself because the photo is at least thirty years old and because, although I know she knows I went through her drawer, I just don't want to bring it up.

"Wow, she's a beautiful baby," I say, and tears flow. She *is* beautiful. They both are. They are more beautiful than the whole universe, and I cry uncontrollably from pure joy and pure love.

Astrid crouches next to us and lifts my head, wiping my tears. Then, she leans in and kisses me on the lips.

"You're gonna be okay, Nick," she says. "*We're* gonna be okay, *Baby.*"

She kisses me again, puts her hand on my cheek, stands up and walks away.

Yeshe licks my face once more and trots after her.

I *know* the method now. It's to worship *them* like De La Soul — all *three* of them.

And now I'm just standing here, and I realise you've come this far with me, and I want to thank you for that. I know I'm a bastard to be around at times.

This could have been a really shit ending, especially if I had splattered off that building. Sure, the story would have been shorter, which would have given you more time to make the Christmas dinner and prepare the egg nog and all that, but then I'd be dead instead of sitting here in the euphoric light of shite.

Do me a favour and put on that Van Morrison song, *Into the Mystic.* I'm talking about the recorded version, not the live one.

Listen to it while you join me for this last page, would you?

You don't have to, but you know me. You know I usually fuck up these poetic moments, and I'm determined not to do that this time. I need all the help I can get.

I sit back down on the stone wall and look around. It's a beautiful day, and the sun is washing everything with light. I look back at the beautiful yellow flower, and it's normal again. It's just a yellow flower, and both the flower and I are okay with that. I laugh for no reason, then pull the small red book out of my pocket again — *Zen Mind, Beginner's Mind,* and I open it to a random page:

When you are practising zazen, do not try to stop your think-ing. Let it stop by itself. If something comes into your mind, let it come in, and let it go out. It will not stay long. When you try to stop your thinking, it means you are bothered by it. Do not be bothered by anything.

Do not be bothered by anything.
Do not be bothered by anything.
Do not be bothered by —

The person who can freely acknowledge that life is full of difficulties can be free because they are acknowledging the nature of life — that it can't be much else.

This sun. This euphoria. All this bliss. It feels *unbalanced* like I'm just feeding the intensity of the next damn crash.

You spend your life pushing toward the bliss, but the older you get, the more you watch it swing between the darkness and the light.

Isn't it time we accepted that the light can't last and that the harder we push for it, the greater the pain when it swings back into the darkness? When I say *we*, I mean *me*, obviously.

And yeah, I know it can't be that easy like I'm now a wise Zen master like Suzuki Roshi or Astrid — and it isn't.

This ending — this poetic ending — isn't what you think. It's not a fucking fairy tale because *life* isn't a fucking fairy tale. The sun of lust and euphoria masks my illness — my dark condition.

I don't know if I'll be a good father, lover, or even human. It's easy to think you will be when you are drenched in bliss. But now, as I feel the depression creep back in for no reason whatsoever, I look down at the same yellow flower and it seems — *empty*.

This is a good ending. You might think I fucked it up again, but I didn't. It's poetry. It's just more balanced now — all that yin-yang crap.

I'm not going to be that tantric guy with the dreadlocks. I'm Nick Conrad, ex-con, onion cutter and voluminous spunker, and I think I'm alright with that — for now.

There's a storm brewing. But this time, I'm ready for it, I think.

I pick the yellow flower and pull off the bright petals one by one. Then I split up the seeds from the stalk until there's nothing left.

Where is your damn yellow flower of bliss now?

Emptiness.

A gust of wind blows, and a dark cloud covers the sun, and before you can say, *fuck it*, it's raining again.

A Message from Frank T Bird

First of all, thanks a million for buying this — unless you stole it, in which case, thanks for stealing it, you dodgy prick.

I'd buy you a milkshake to say thanks, but with the scanty royalty I get from the sale, that would make the whole thing a negative investment on my part, and I'll be fucked if I'm going to pay you to read my books since I've got three *bon vivant* cats to feed.

Now, please, please go and write a review at the place you bought it, or I'll send my cousin Henry with the big fists over to break into your car and nick your gerbil skin seat covers.

But seriously, thanks again, mate.

All the best,

Frank T Bird

Melbourne, May 2023